GET IN THE GAME

VAULTING TO VICTORY

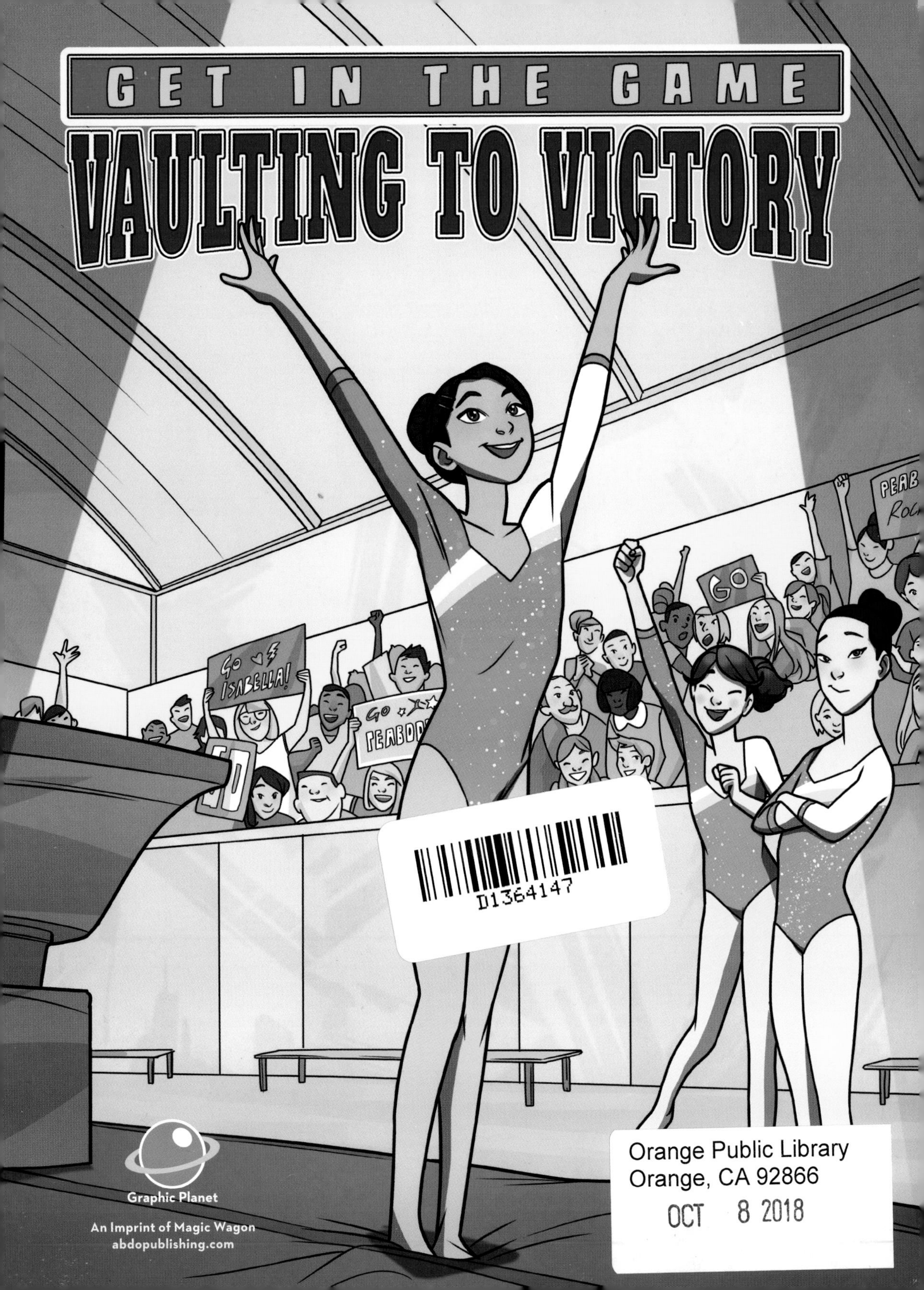
GO ISABELLA!
GO

Graphic Planet
An Imprint of Magic Wagon
abdopublishing.com

abdopublishing.com

Published by Magic Wagon, a division of ABDO, PO Box 398166, Minneapolis, Minnesota 55439.
Copyright © 2019 by Abdo Consulting Group, Inc. International copyrights reserved in all countries.
No part of this book may be reproduced in any form without written permission from the publisher.
Graphic Planet™ is a trademark and logo of Magic Wagon.

Printed in the United States of America, North Mankato, Minnesota.
052018
092018

THIS BOOK CONTAINS
RECYCLED MATERIALS

Written by Bill Yu
Pencils by Paola Amormino
Inks by Renato Siragusa
Colored by Tiziana Musmeci
Lettered by Kathryn S. Renta
Card Illustrations by Emanuele Cardillo and Gabriele Cracolici (Grafimated)
Layout and design by Pejee Calanog of Glass House Graphics and Christina Doffing of ABDO
Editorial supervision by David Campiti
Edited by Salvatore Di Marco and Giovanni Spadaro (Grafimated Cartoon)
Packaged by Glass House Graphics
Art Directed by Candice Keimig
Editorial Support by Tamara L. Britton

Library of Congress Control Number: 2018932637

Publisher's Cataloging-in-Publication Data

Names: Yu, Bill, author. | Amormino, Paola, illustrator. | Siragusa, Renato, illustrator.
Title: Vaulting to victory / by Bill Yu; illustrated by Paola Amormino and Renato Siragusa.
Description: Minneapolis, Minnesota : Magic Wagon, 2019. | Series: Get in the game
Summary: Isabella Clemente is a champion all-around gymnast. After a summer at gymnastics camp, she
   is looking forward to winning a national championship. But then the current national champion
   transfers to Peabody! Isabella sees Morgan as a rival. Can she get past this when Morgan offers
   Isabella help?
Identifiers: ISBN 9781532132988 (lib.bdg.) | ISBN 9781532133121 (ebook) |
   ISBN 9781532133190 (Read-to-me ebook)
Subjects: LCSH: Gymnastics--Juvenile fiction. | Sports camps--Juvenile fiction. | Sports rivalries--
   Juvenile fiction. | Self-reliance in adolescence--Juvenile fiction. | Graphic novels--Juvenile fiction.
Classification: DDC 741.5--dc23

CONTENTS

VAULTING TO VICTORY

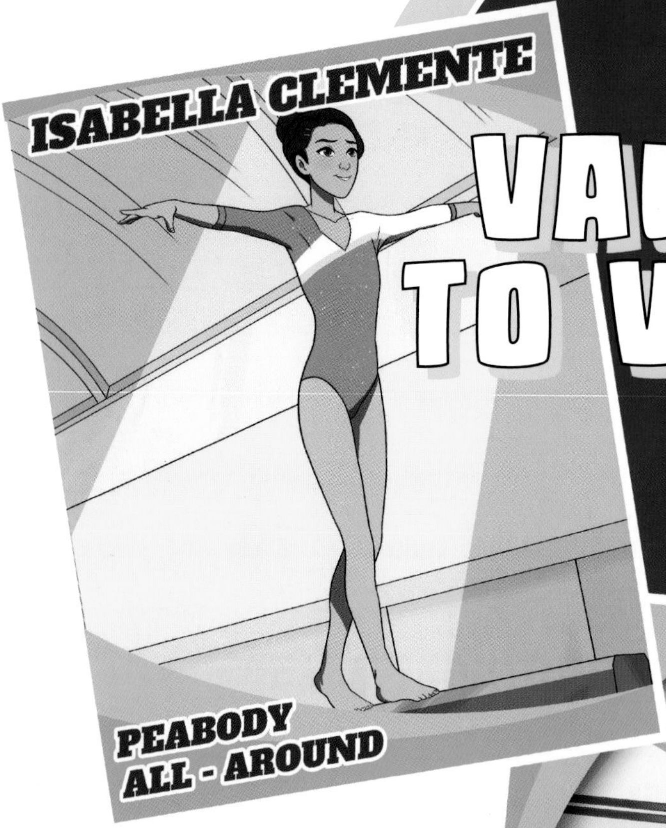
ISABELLA CLEMENTE
PEABODY
ALL - AROUND

ISABELLA CLEMENTE

Isabella Clemente, All-Around

Isabella Clemente has been the captain of the gymnastics team for the past two years. She is a strong all-around gymnast who specializes in the balance beam.

RECORD

	GOLD	SILVER	BRONZE
BALANCE BEAM	0	2	0
FLOOR EXERCISE	0	2	0
UNEVEN BARS	0	2	0
VAULT	0	1	1

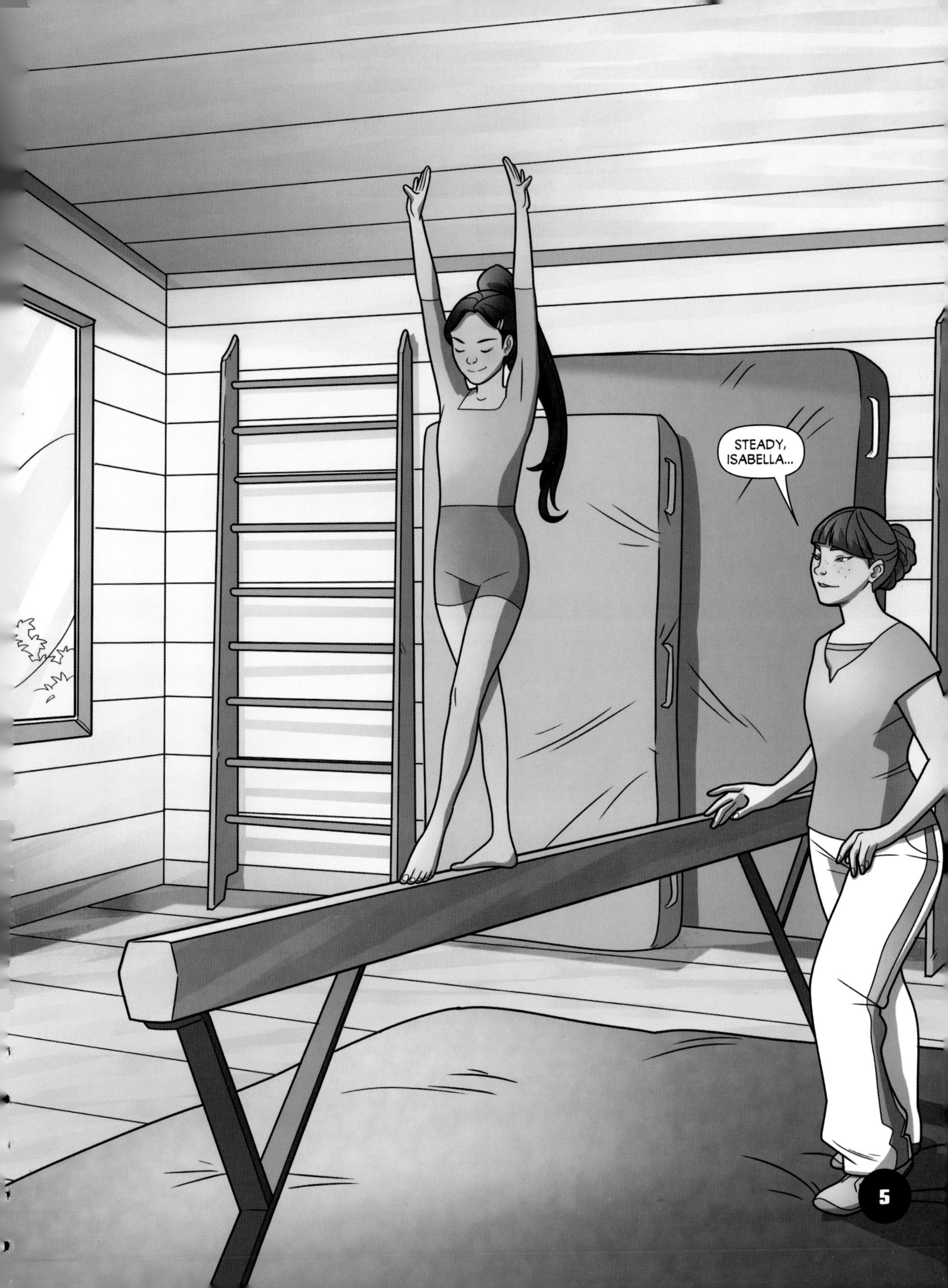
STEADY,
ISABELLA...

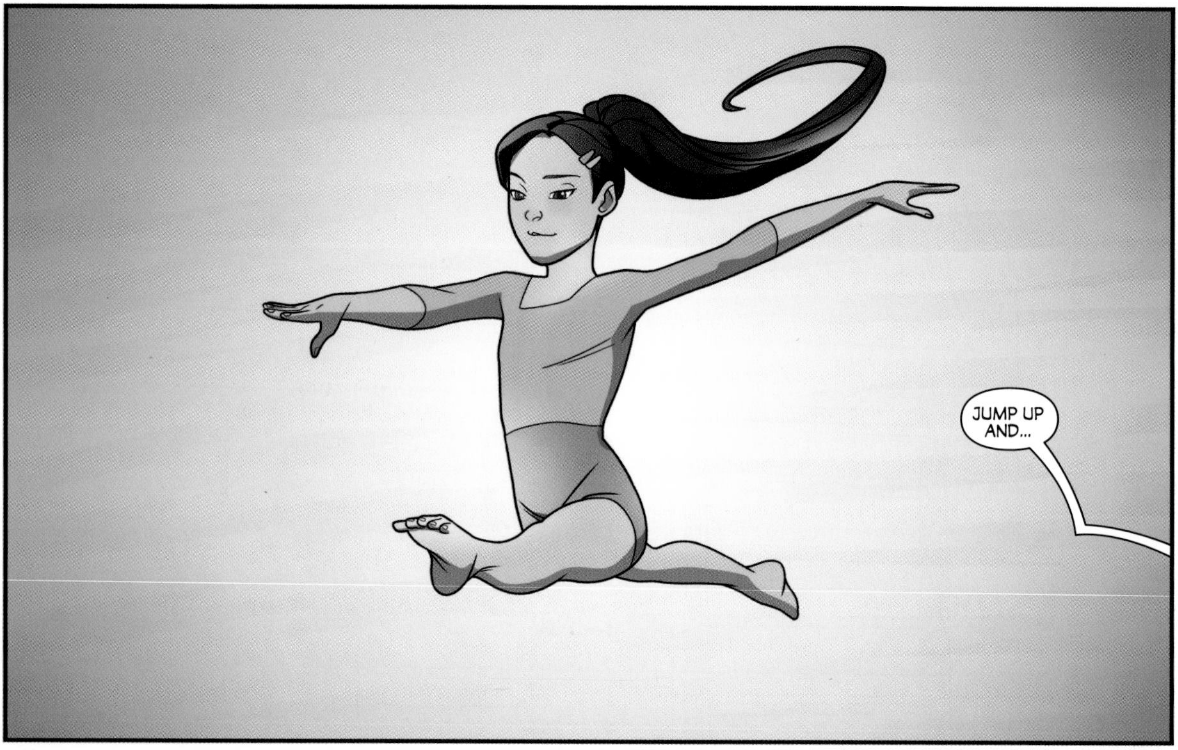
JUMP UP AND...

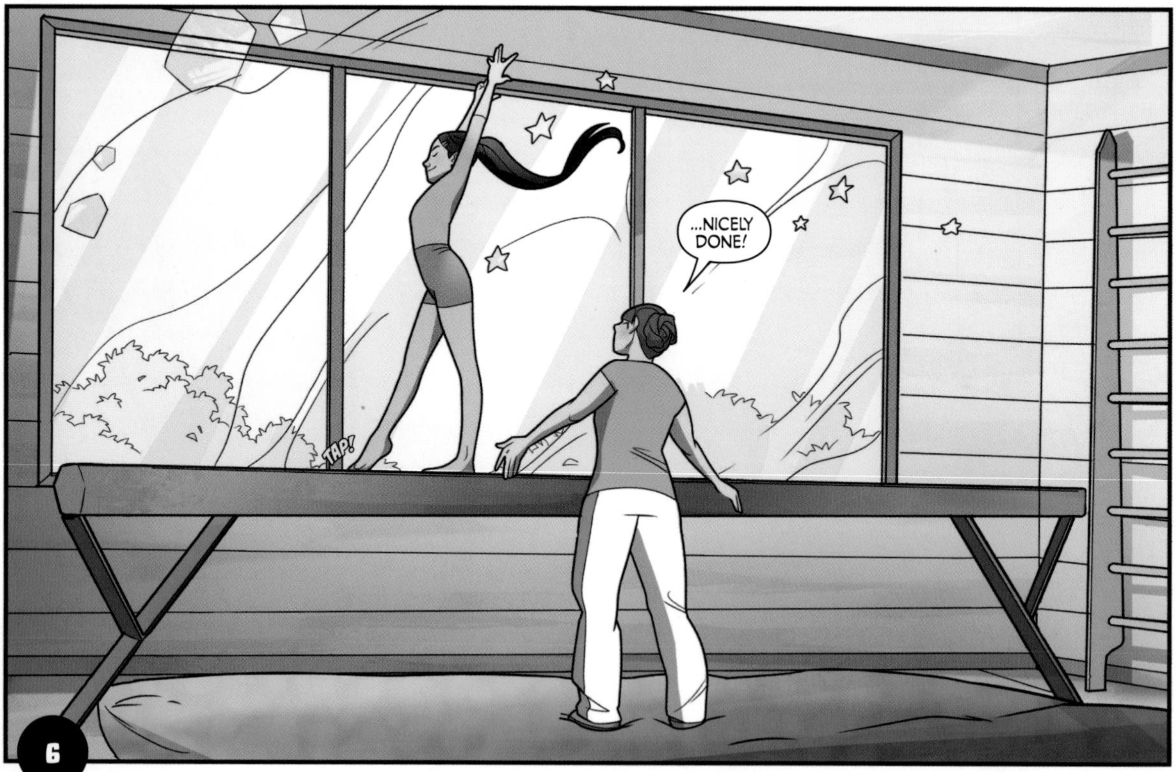
...NICELY DONE!
TAP!

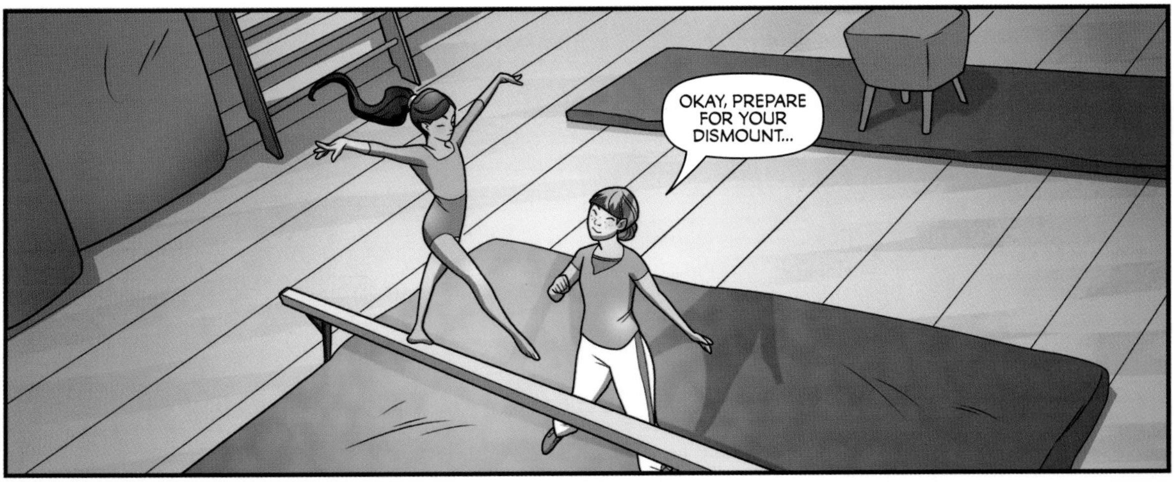
OKAY, PREPARE FOR YOUR DISMOUNT...

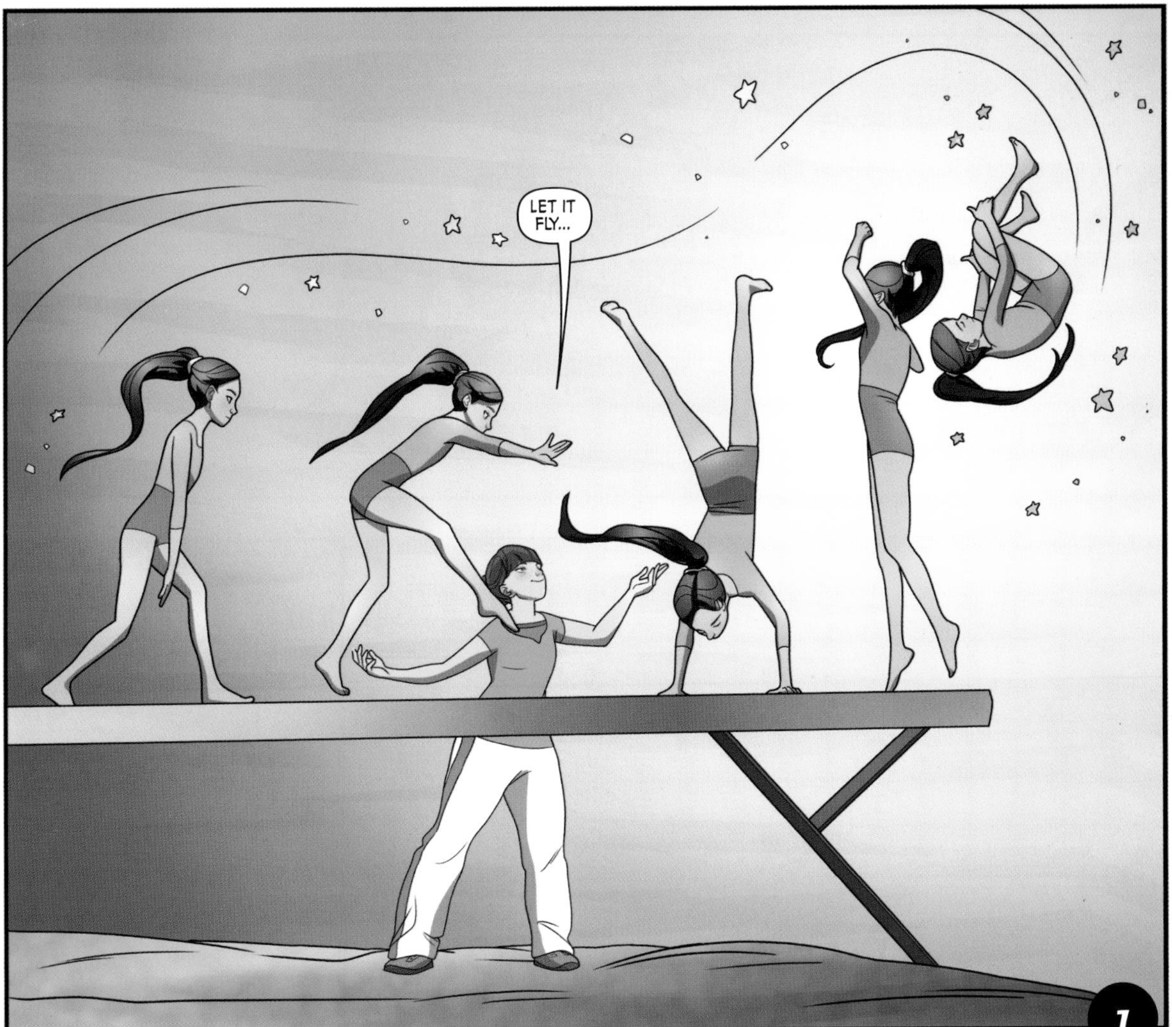
LET IT FLY...

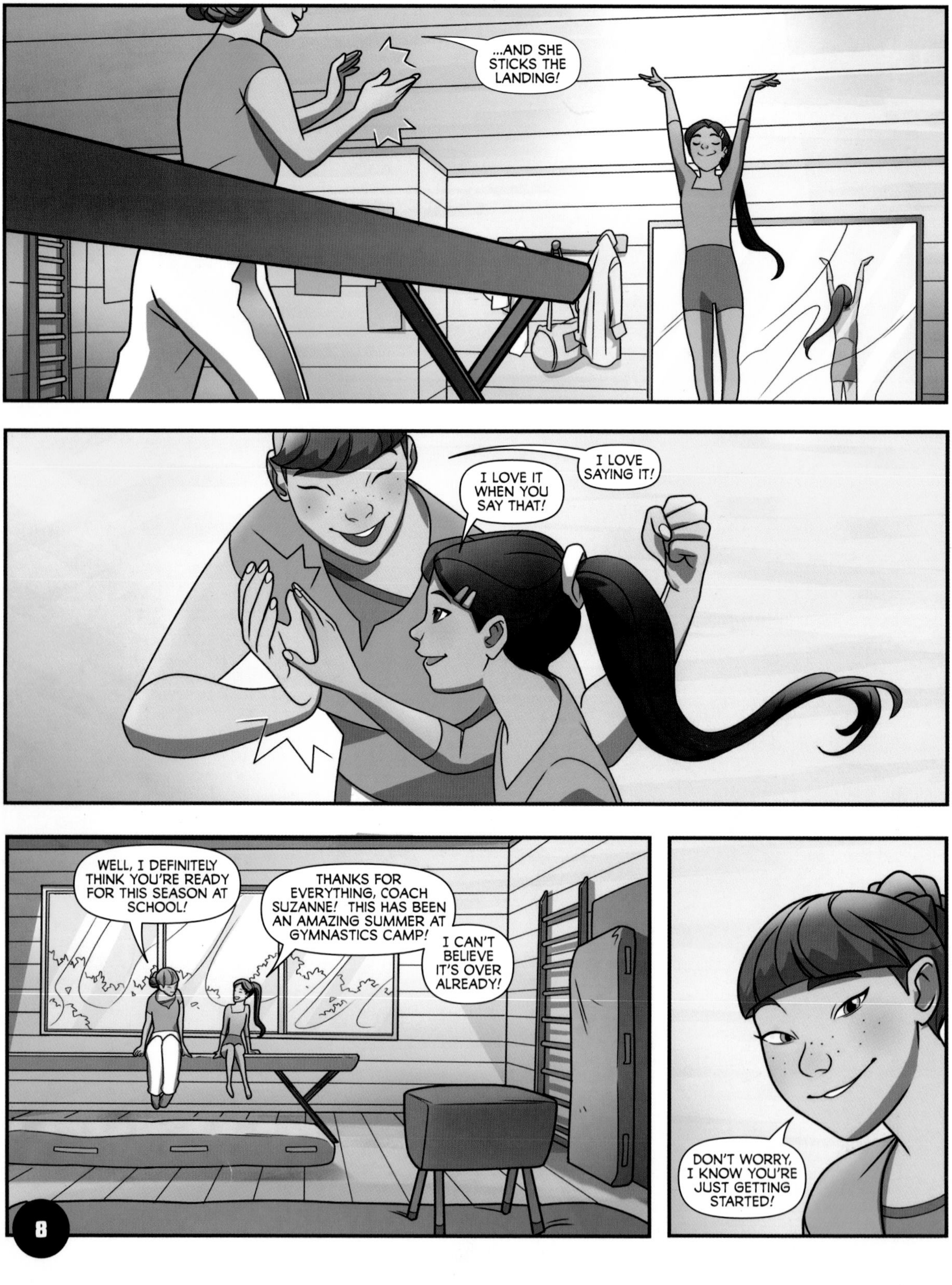
...AND SHE STICKS THE LANDING!
I LOVE IT WHEN YOU SAY THAT!
I LOVE SAYING IT!
WELL, I DEFINITELY THINK YOU'RE READY FOR THIS SEASON AT SCHOOL!
THANKS FOR EVERYTHING, COACH SUZANNE! THIS HAS BEEN AN AMAZING SUMMER AT GYMNASTICS CAMP!
I CAN'T BELIEVE IT'S OVER ALREADY!
DON'T WORRY, I KNOW YOU'RE JUST GETTING STARTED!

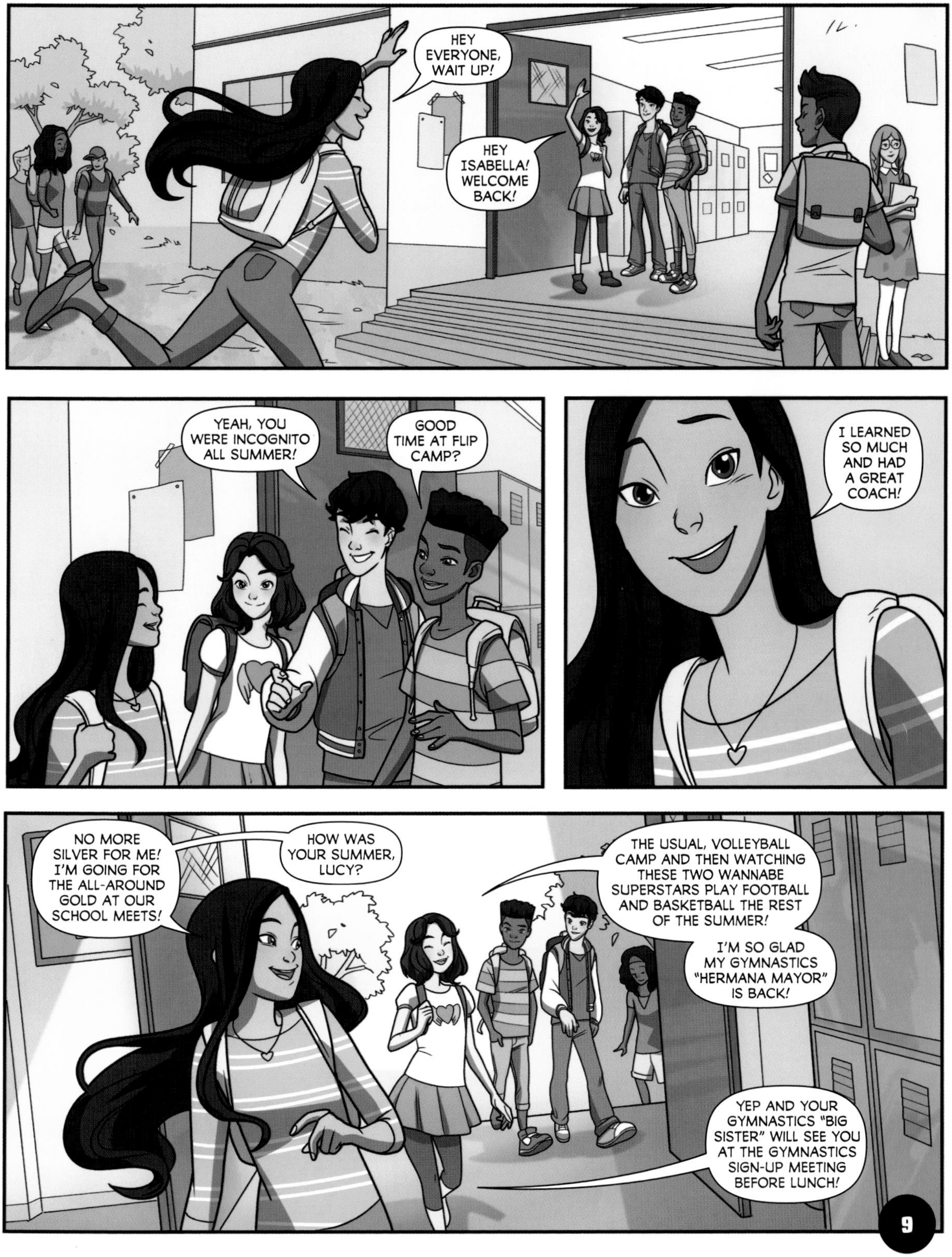
HEY EVERYONE, WAIT UP!
HEY ISABELLA! WELCOME BACK!
YEAH, YOU WERE INCOGNITO ALL SUMMER!
GOOD TIME AT FLIP CAMP?
I LEARNED SO MUCH AND HAD A GREAT COACH!
NO MORE SILVER FOR ME! I'M GOING FOR THE ALL-AROUND GOLD AT OUR SCHOOL MEETS!
HOW WAS YOUR SUMMER, LUCY?
THE USUAL, VOLLEYBALL CAMP AND THEN WATCHING THESE TWO WANNABE SUPERSTARS PLAY FOOTBALL AND BASKETBALL THE REST OF THE SUMMER!
I'M SO GLAD MY GYMNASTICS "HERMANA MAYOR" IS BACK!
YEP AND YOUR GYMNASTICS "BIG SISTER" WILL SEE YOU AT THE GYMNASTICS SIGN-UP MEETING BEFORE LUNCH!

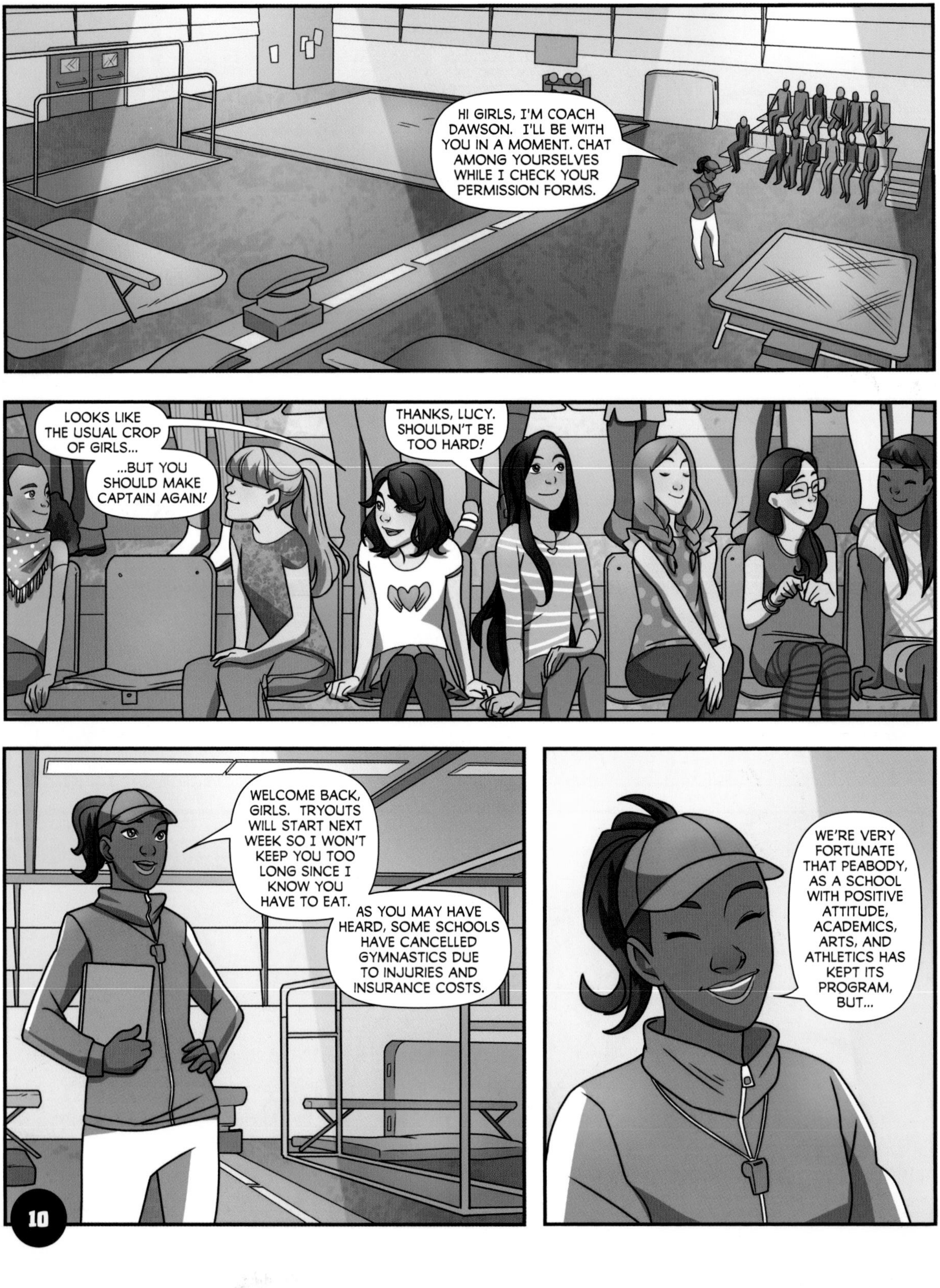
HI GIRLS, I'M COACH DAWSON. I'LL BE WITH YOU IN A MOMENT. CHAT AMONG YOURSELVES WHILE I CHECK YOUR PERMISSION FORMS.
LOOKS LIKE THE USUAL CROP OF GIRLS...
...BUT YOU SHOULD MAKE CAPTAIN AGAIN!
THANKS, LUCY. SHOULDN'T BE TOO HARD!
WELCOME BACK, GIRLS. TRYOUTS WILL START NEXT WEEK SO I WON'T KEEP YOU TOO LONG SINCE I KNOW YOU HAVE TO EAT.
AS YOU MAY HAVE HEARD, SOME SCHOOLS HAVE CANCELLED GYMNASTICS DUE TO INJURIES AND INSURANCE COSTS.
WE'RE VERY FORTUNATE THAT PEABODY, AS A SCHOOL WITH POSITIVE ATTITUDE, ACADEMICS, ARTS, AND ATHLETICS HAS KEPT ITS PROGRAM, BUT...

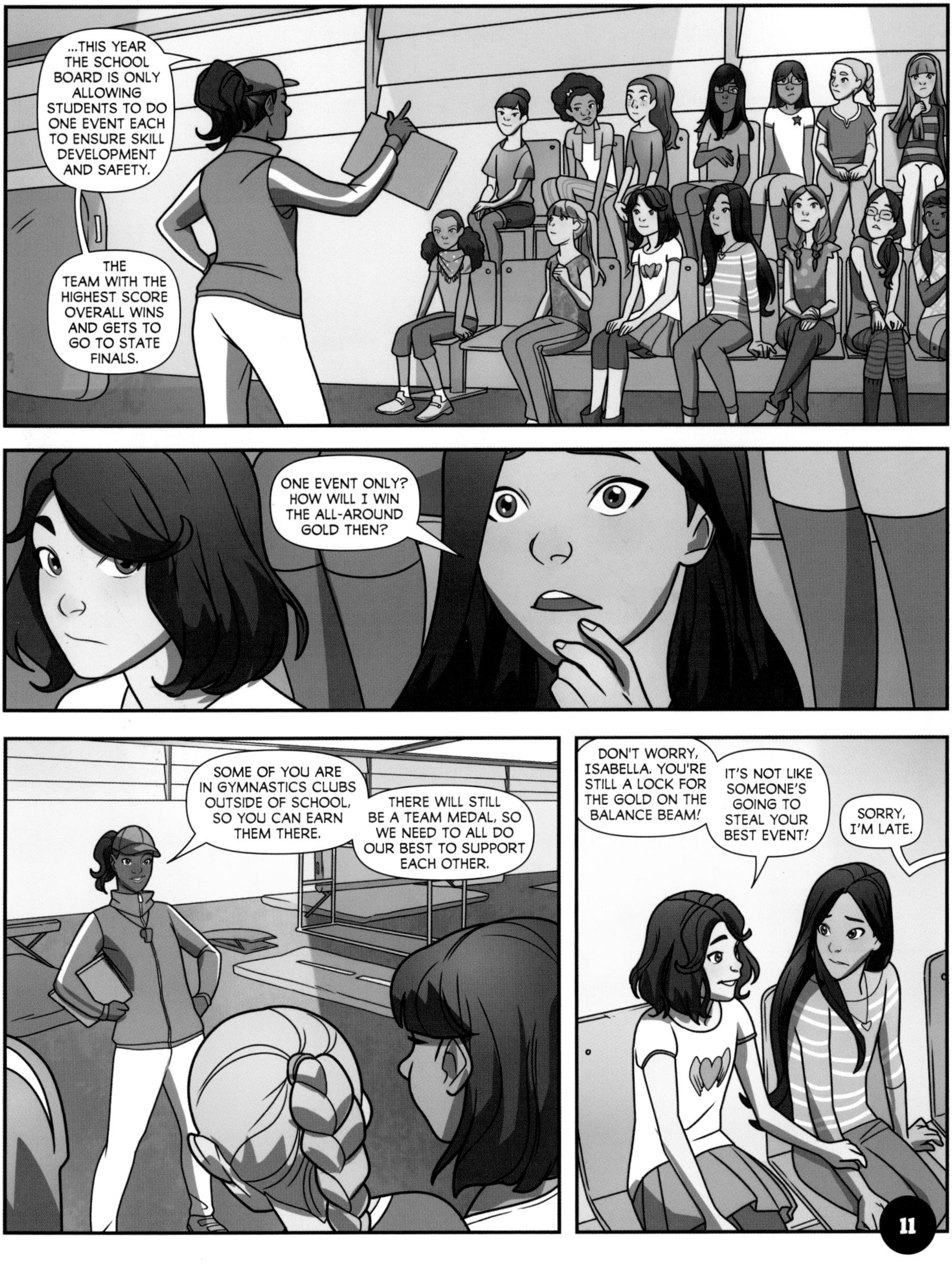
...THIS YEAR THE SCHOOL BOARD IS ONLY ALLOWING STUDENTS TO DO ONE EVENT EACH TO ENSURE SKILL DEVELOPMENT AND SAFETY.
THE TEAM WITH THE HIGHEST SCORE OVERALL WINS AND GETS TO GO TO STATE FINALS.
ONE EVENT ONLY? HOW WILL I WIN THE ALL-AROUND GOLD THEN?
SOME OF YOU ARE IN GYMNASTICS CLUBS OUTSIDE OF SCHOOL, SO YOU CAN EARN THEM THERE.
THERE WILL STILL BE A TEAM MEDAL, SO WE NEED TO ALL DO OUR BEST TO SUPPORT EACH OTHER.
DON'T WORRY, ISABELLA. YOU'RE STILL A LOCK FOR THE GOLD ON THE BALANCE BEAM!
IT'S NOT LIKE SOMEONE'S GOING TO STEAL YOUR BEST EVENT!
SORRY, I'M LATE.

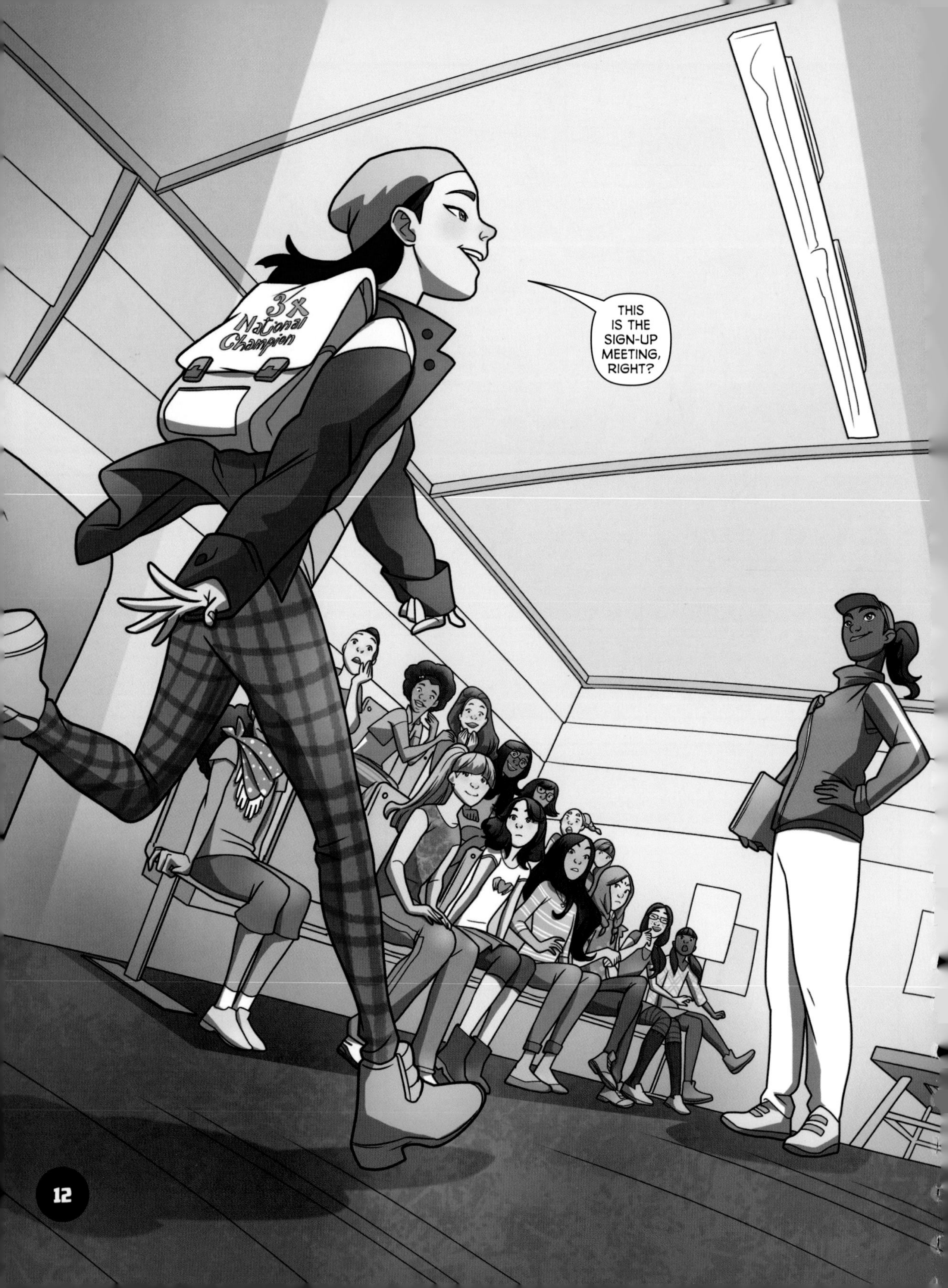
3x National Champion
THIS IS THE SIGN-UP MEETING, RIGHT?

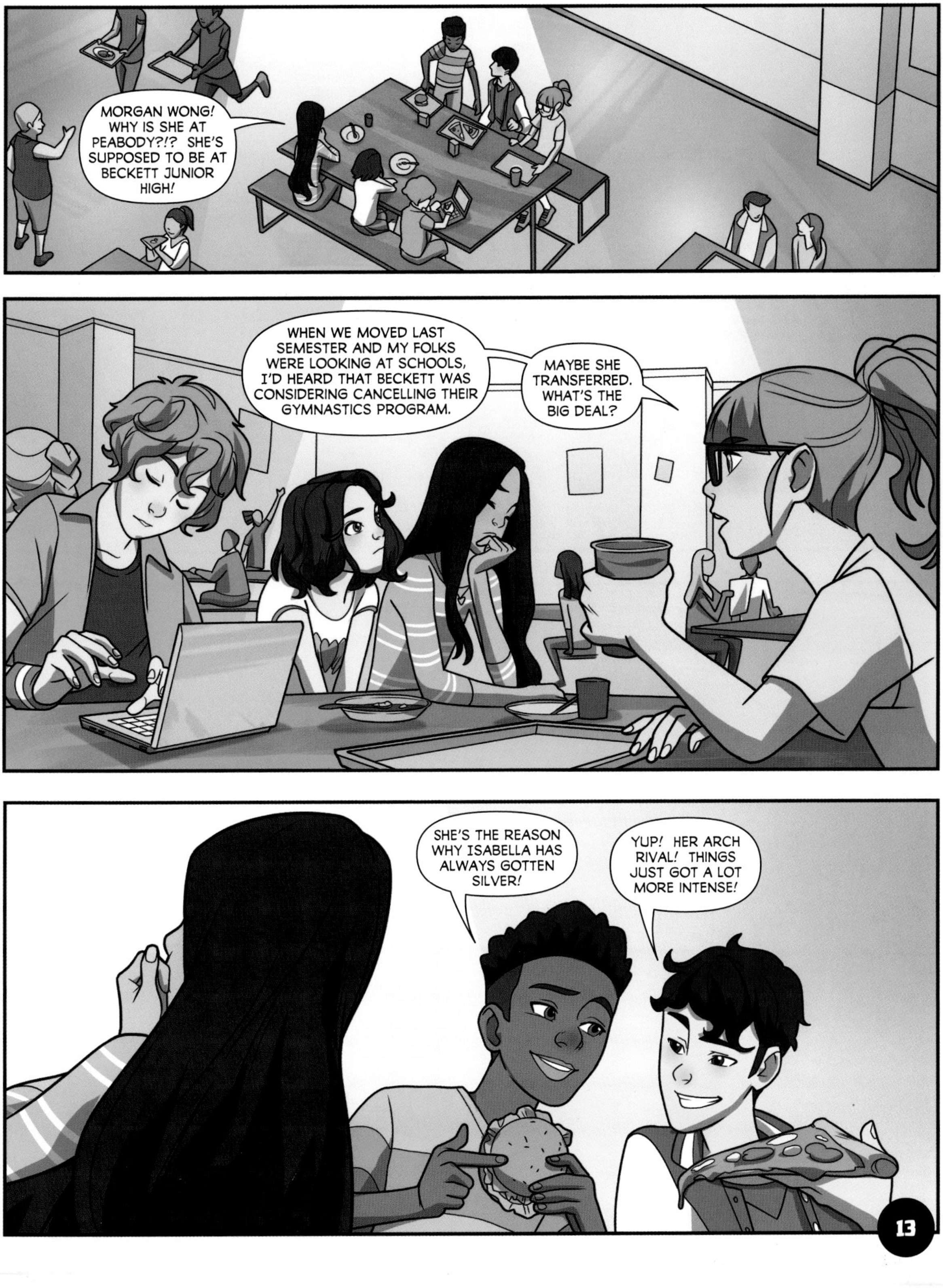
MORGAN WONG! WHY IS SHE AT PEABODY?!? SHE'S SUPPOSED TO BE AT BECKETT JUNIOR HIGH!
WHEN WE MOVED LAST SEMESTER AND MY FOLKS WERE LOOKING AT SCHOOLS, I'D HEARD THAT BECKETT WAS CONSIDERING CANCELLING THEIR GYMNASTICS PROGRAM.
MAYBE SHE TRANSFERRED. WHAT'S THE BIG DEAL?
SHE'S THE REASON WHY ISABELLA HAS ALWAYS GOTTEN SILVER!
YUP! HER ARCH RIVAL! THINGS JUST GOT A LOT MORE INTENSE!

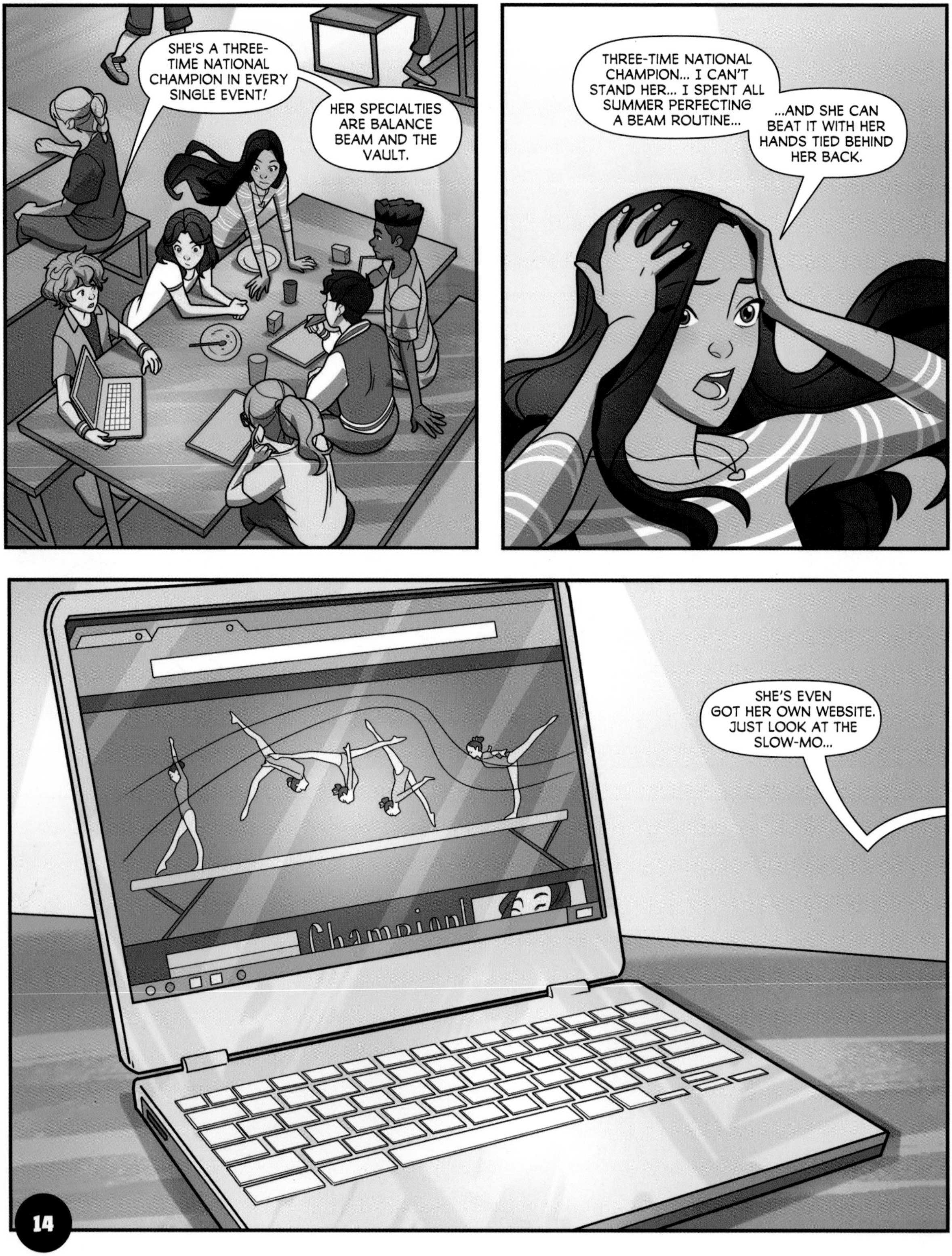
SHE'S A THREE-TIME NATIONAL CHAMPION IN EVERY SINGLE EVENT!
HER SPECIALTIES ARE BALANCE BEAM AND THE VAULT.
THREE-TIME NATIONAL CHAMPION... I CAN'T STAND HER... I SPENT ALL SUMMER PERFECTING A BEAM ROUTINE...
...AND SHE CAN BEAT IT WITH HER HANDS TIED BEHIND HER BACK.
Champion!
SHE'S EVEN GOT HER OWN WEBSITE. JUST LOOK AT THE SLOW-MO...

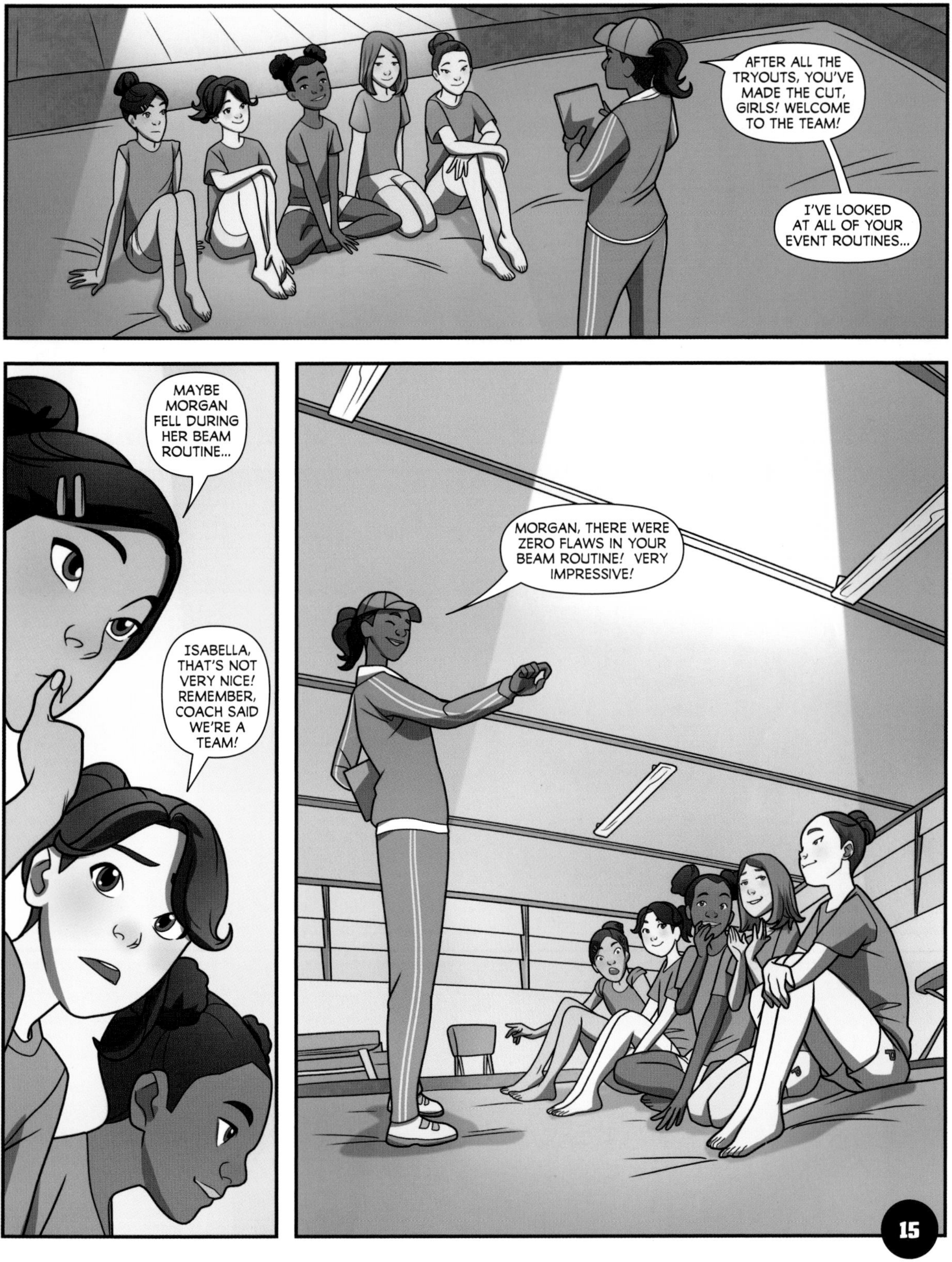
AFTER ALL THE TRYOUTS, YOU'VE MADE THE CUT, GIRLS! WELCOME TO THE TEAM!
I'VE LOOKED AT ALL OF YOUR EVENT ROUTINES...
MAYBE MORGAN FELL DURING HER BEAM ROUTINE...
ISABELLA, THAT'S NOT VERY NICE! REMEMBER, COACH SAID WE'RE A TEAM!
MORGAN, THERE WERE ZERO FLAWS IN YOUR BEAM ROUTINE! VERY IMPRESSIVE!

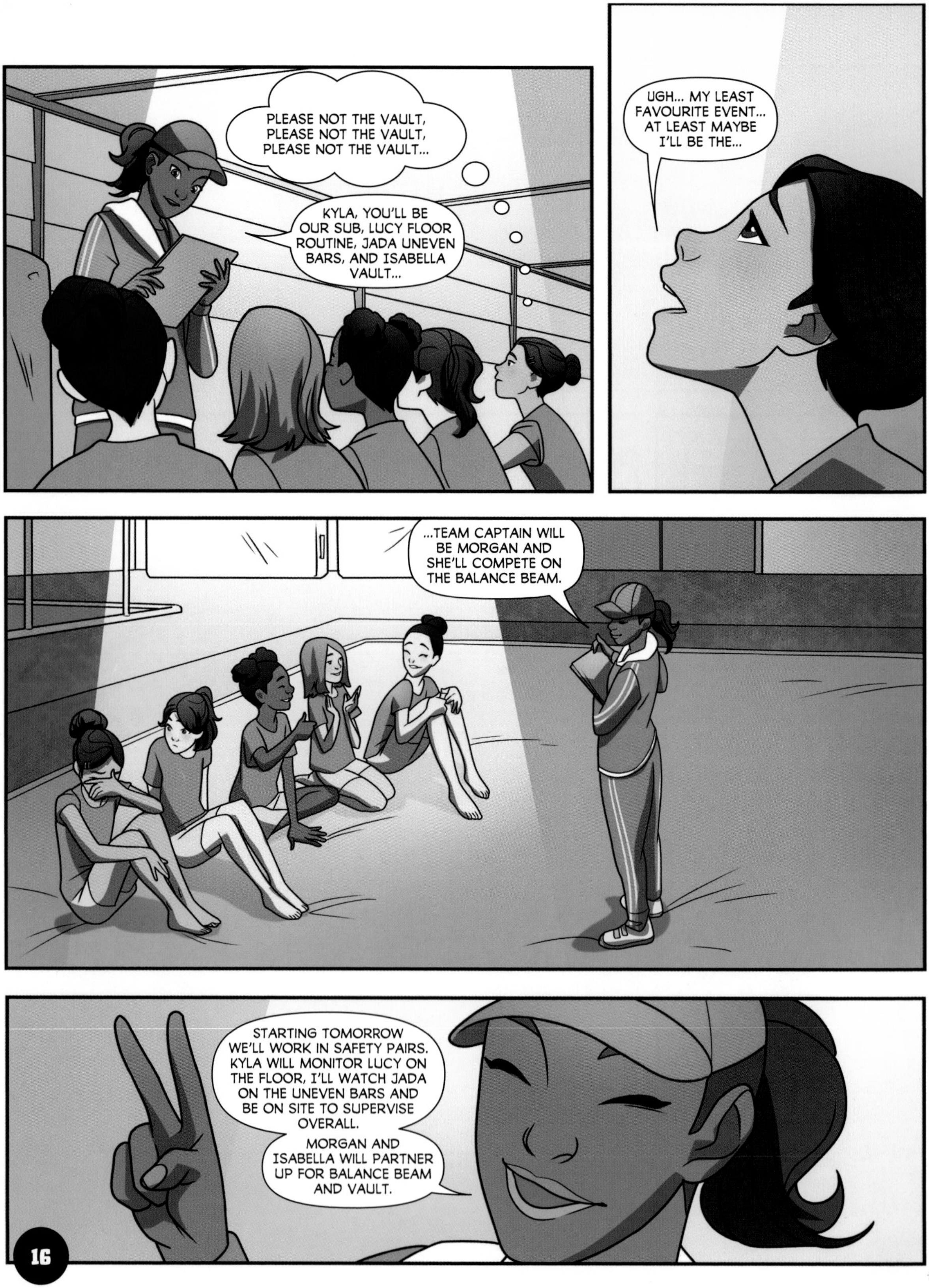
PLEASE NOT THE VAULT, PLEASE NOT THE VAULT, PLEASE NOT THE VAULT...
KYLA, YOU'LL BE OUR SUB, LUCY FLOOR ROUTINE, JADA UNEVEN BARS, AND ISABELLA VAULT...
UGH... MY LEAST FAVOURITE EVENT... AT LEAST MAYBE I'LL BE THE...
...TEAM CAPTAIN WILL BE MORGAN AND SHE'LL COMPETE ON THE BALANCE BEAM.
STARTING TOMORROW WE'LL WORK IN SAFETY PAIRS. KYLA WILL MONITOR LUCY ON THE FLOOR, I'LL WATCH JADA ON THE UNEVEN BARS AND BE ON SITE TO SUPERVISE OVERALL.
MORGAN AND ISABELLA WILL PARTNER UP FOR BALANCE BEAM AND VAULT.

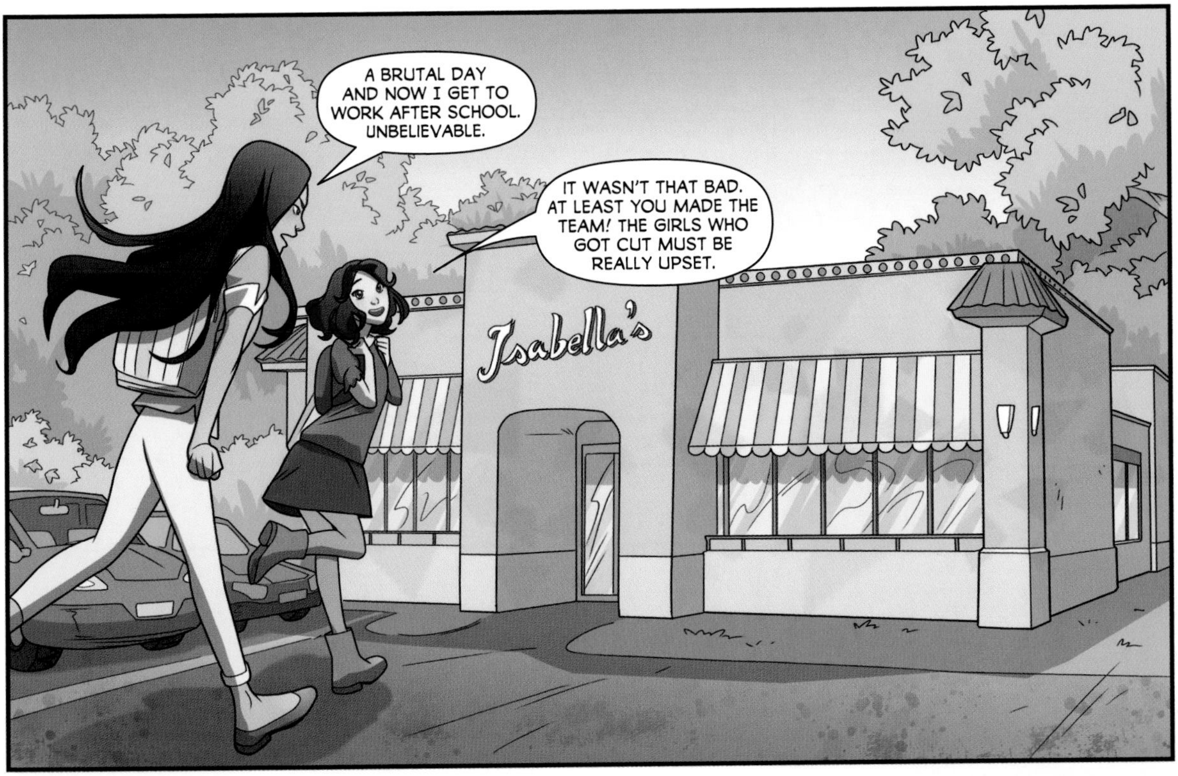
A BRUTAL DAY AND NOW I GET TO WORK AFTER SCHOOL. UNBELIEVABLE.
IT WASN'T THAT BAD. AT LEAST YOU MADE THE TEAM! THE GIRLS WHO GOT CUT MUST BE REALLY UPSET.
Isabella's

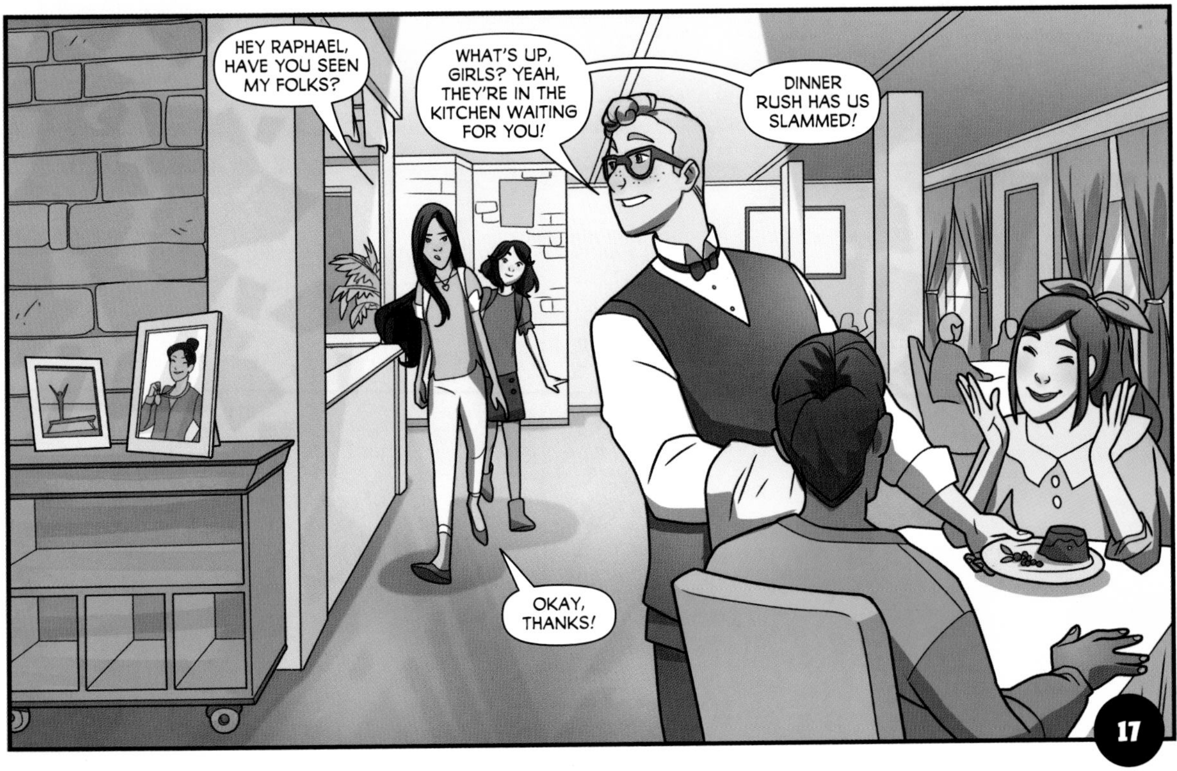
HEY RAPHAEL, HAVE YOU SEEN MY FOLKS?
WHAT'S UP, GIRLS? YEAH, THEY'RE IN THE KITCHEN WAITING FOR YOU!
DINNER RUSH HAS US SLAMMED!
OKAY, THANKS!

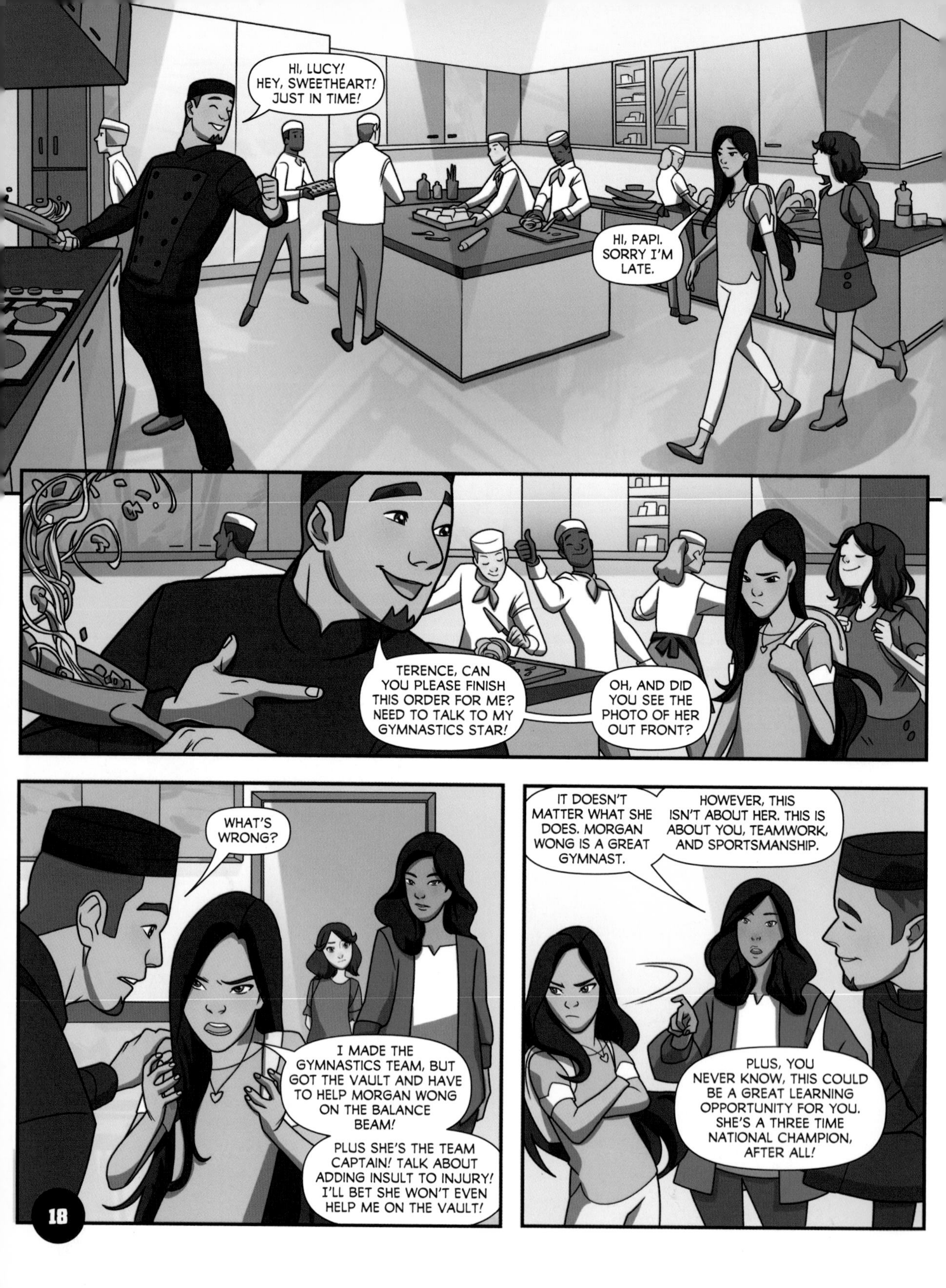
HI, LUCY! HEY, SWEETHEART! JUST IN TIME!
HI, PAPI. SORRY I'M LATE.
TERENCE, CAN YOU PLEASE FINISH THIS ORDER FOR ME? NEED TO TALK TO MY GYMNASTICS STAR!
OH, AND DID YOU SEE THE PHOTO OF HER OUT FRONT?
WHAT'S WRONG?
I MADE THE GYMNASTICS TEAM, BUT GOT THE VAULT AND HAVE TO HELP MORGAN WONG ON THE BALANCE BEAM!
PLUS SHE'S THE TEAM CAPTAIN! TALK ABOUT ADDING INSULT TO INJURY! I'LL BET SHE WON'T EVEN HELP ME ON THE VAULT!
IT DOESN'T MATTER WHAT SHE DOES. MORGAN WONG IS A GREAT GYMNAST.
HOWEVER, THIS ISN'T ABOUT HER. THIS IS ABOUT YOU, TEAMWORK, AND SPORTSMANSHIP.
PLUS, YOU NEVER KNOW, THIS COULD BE A GREAT LEARNING OPPORTUNITY FOR YOU. SHE'S A THREE TIME NATIONAL CHAMPION, AFTER ALL!

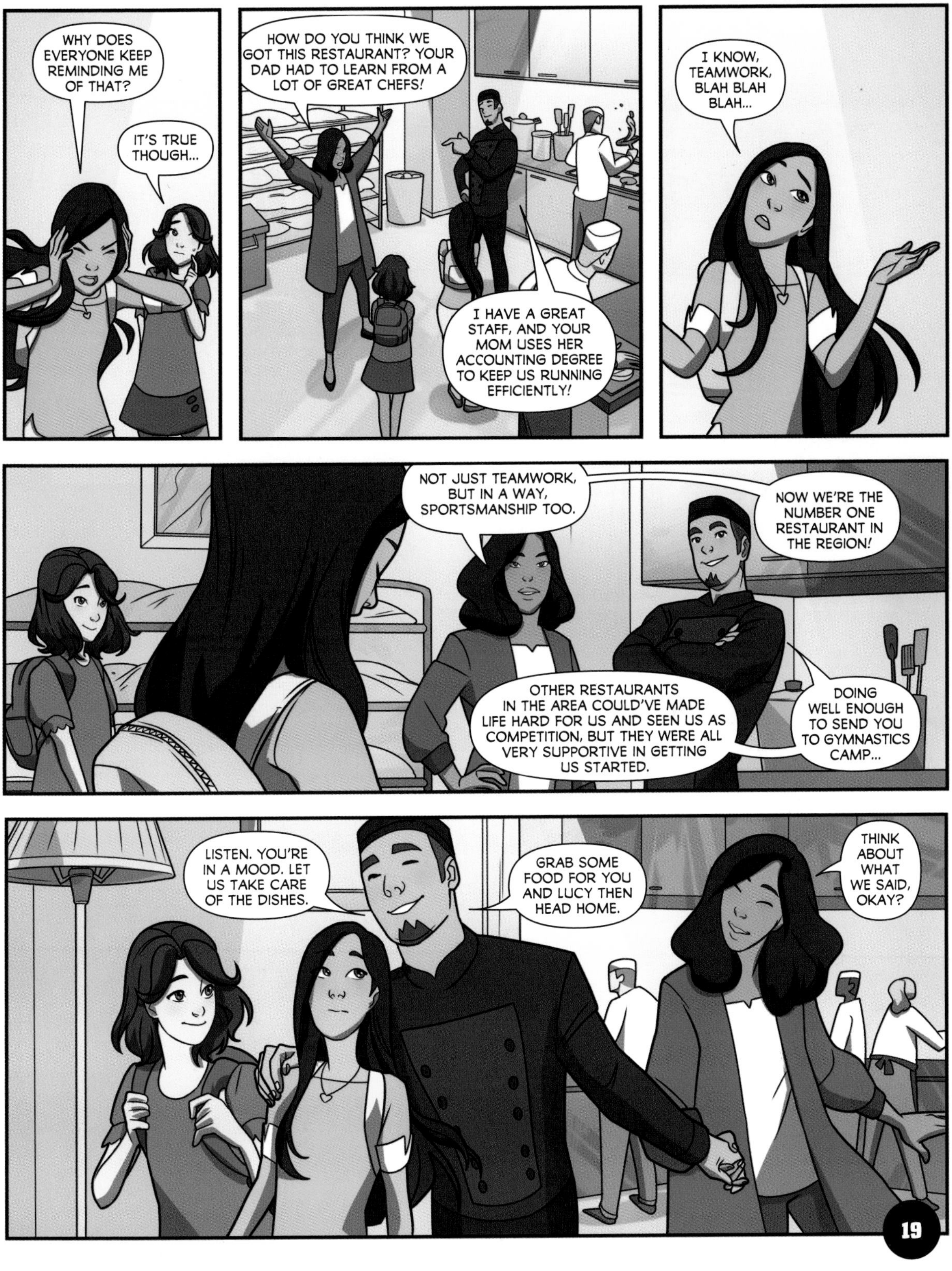

WHY DOES EVERYONE KEEP REMINDING ME OF THAT?
IT'S TRUE THOUGH...
HOW DO YOU THINK WE GOT THIS RESTAURANT? YOUR DAD HAD TO LEARN FROM A LOT OF GREAT CHEFS!
I HAVE A GREAT STAFF, AND YOUR MOM USES HER ACCOUNTING DEGREE TO KEEP US RUNNING EFFICIENTLY!
I KNOW, TEAMWORK, BLAH BLAH BLAH...
NOT JUST TEAMWORK, BUT IN A WAY, SPORTSMANSHIP TOO.
NOW WE'RE THE NUMBER ONE RESTAURANT IN THE REGION!
OTHER RESTAURANTS IN THE AREA COULD'VE MADE LIFE HARD FOR US AND SEEN US AS COMPETITION, BUT THEY WERE ALL VERY SUPPORTIVE IN GETTING US STARTED.
DOING WELL ENOUGH TO SEND YOU TO GYMNASTICS CAMP...
LISTEN. YOU'RE IN A MOOD. LET US TAKE CARE OF THE DISHES.
GRAB SOME FOOD FOR YOU AND LUCY THEN HEAD HOME.
THINK ABOUT WHAT WE SAID, OKAY?

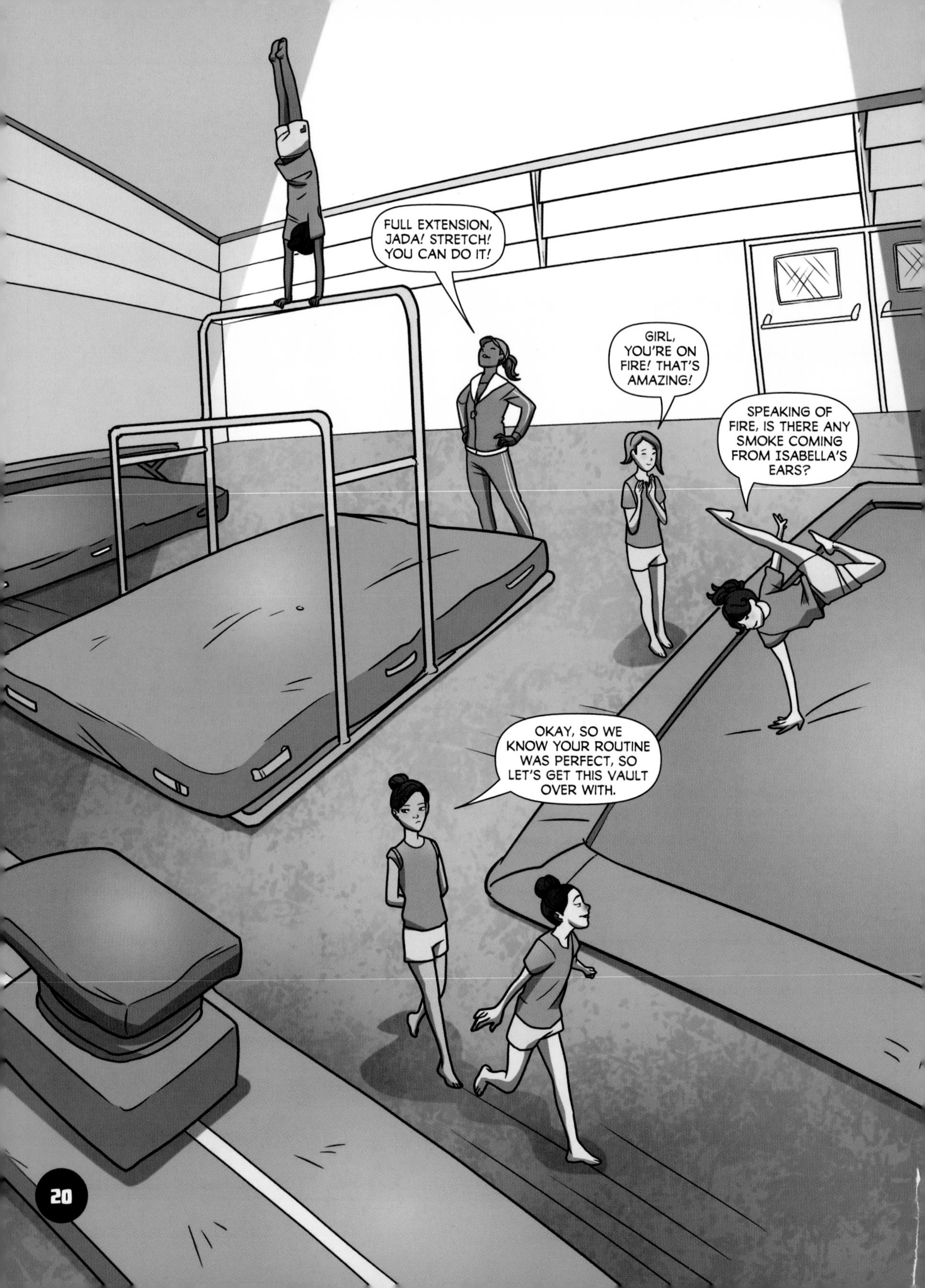
FULL EXTENSION, JADA! STRETCH! YOU CAN DO IT!
GIRL, YOU'RE ON FIRE! THAT'S AMAZING!
SPEAKING OF FIRE, IS THERE ANY SMOKE COMING FROM ISABELLA'S EARS?
OKAY, SO WE KNOW YOUR ROUTINE WAS PERFECT, SO LET'S GET THIS VAULT OVER WITH.

WHAT'S WITH THE DRAMA? WHAT DID I DO TO DESERVE THIS ATTITUDE?
AS IF YOU DIDN'T KNOW!
WHAT?
FORGET IT, NOT LIKE YOU CARE!
I'LL SHOW YOU THE BEST VAULT EVER, MISS THREE-TIME NATIONAL CHAMPION!

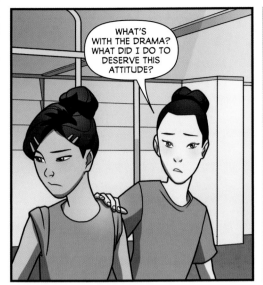

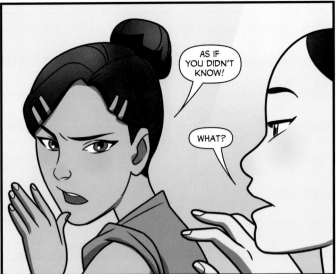

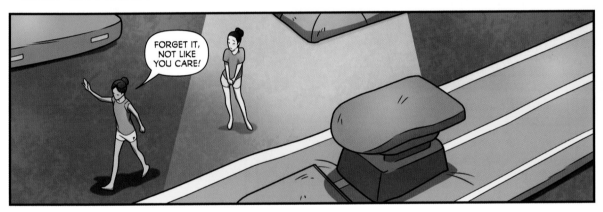

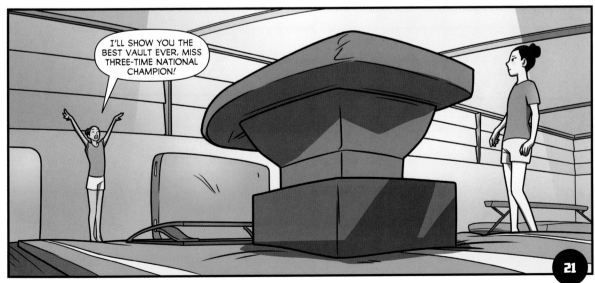

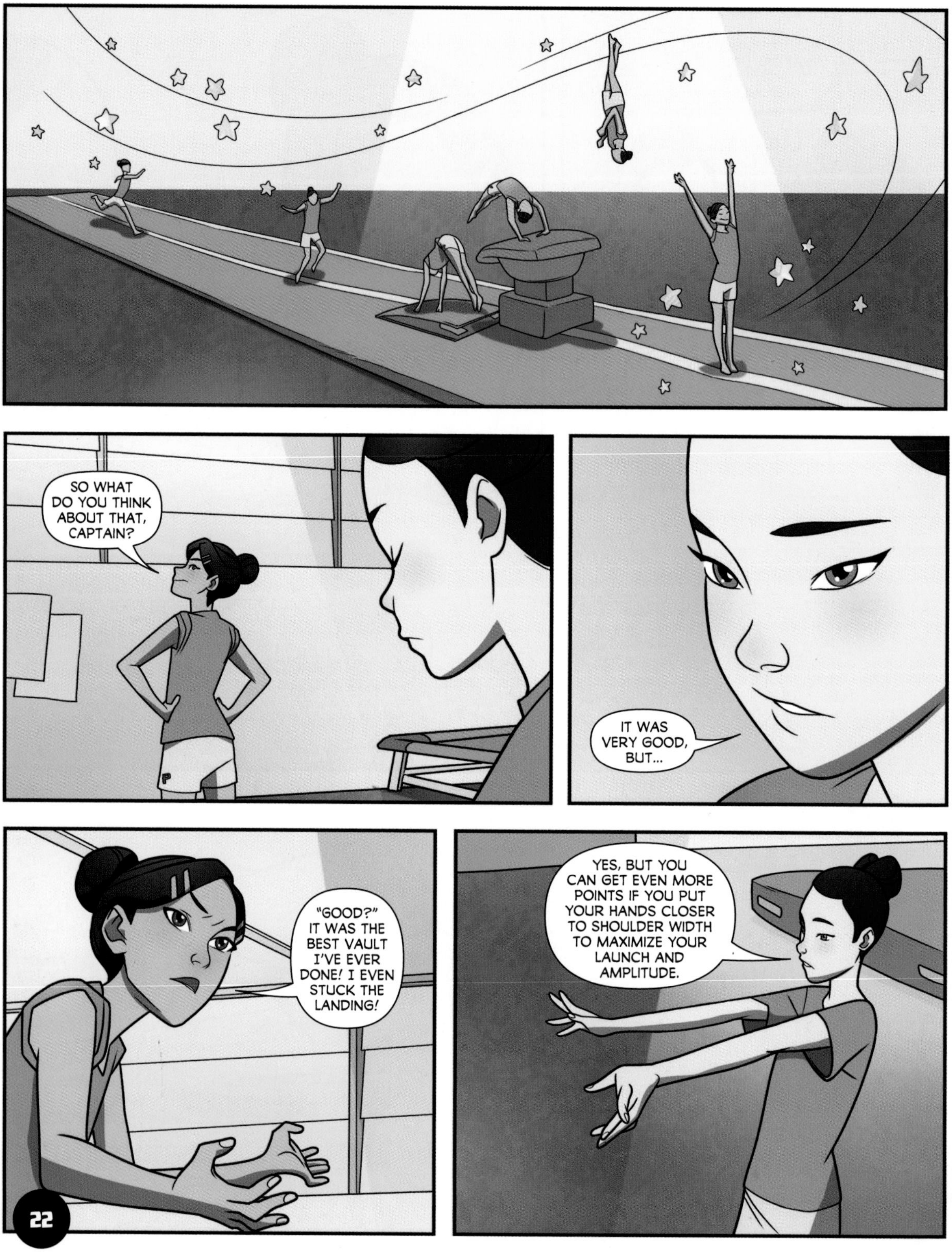
SO WHAT DO YOU THINK ABOUT THAT, CAPTAIN?
IT WAS VERY GOOD, BUT...
"GOOD?" IT WAS THE BEST VAULT I'VE EVER DONE! I EVEN STUCK THE LANDING!
YES, BUT YOU CAN GET EVEN MORE POINTS IF YOU PUT YOUR HANDS CLOSER TO SHOULDER WIDTH TO MAXIMIZE YOUR LAUNCH AND AMPLITUDE.

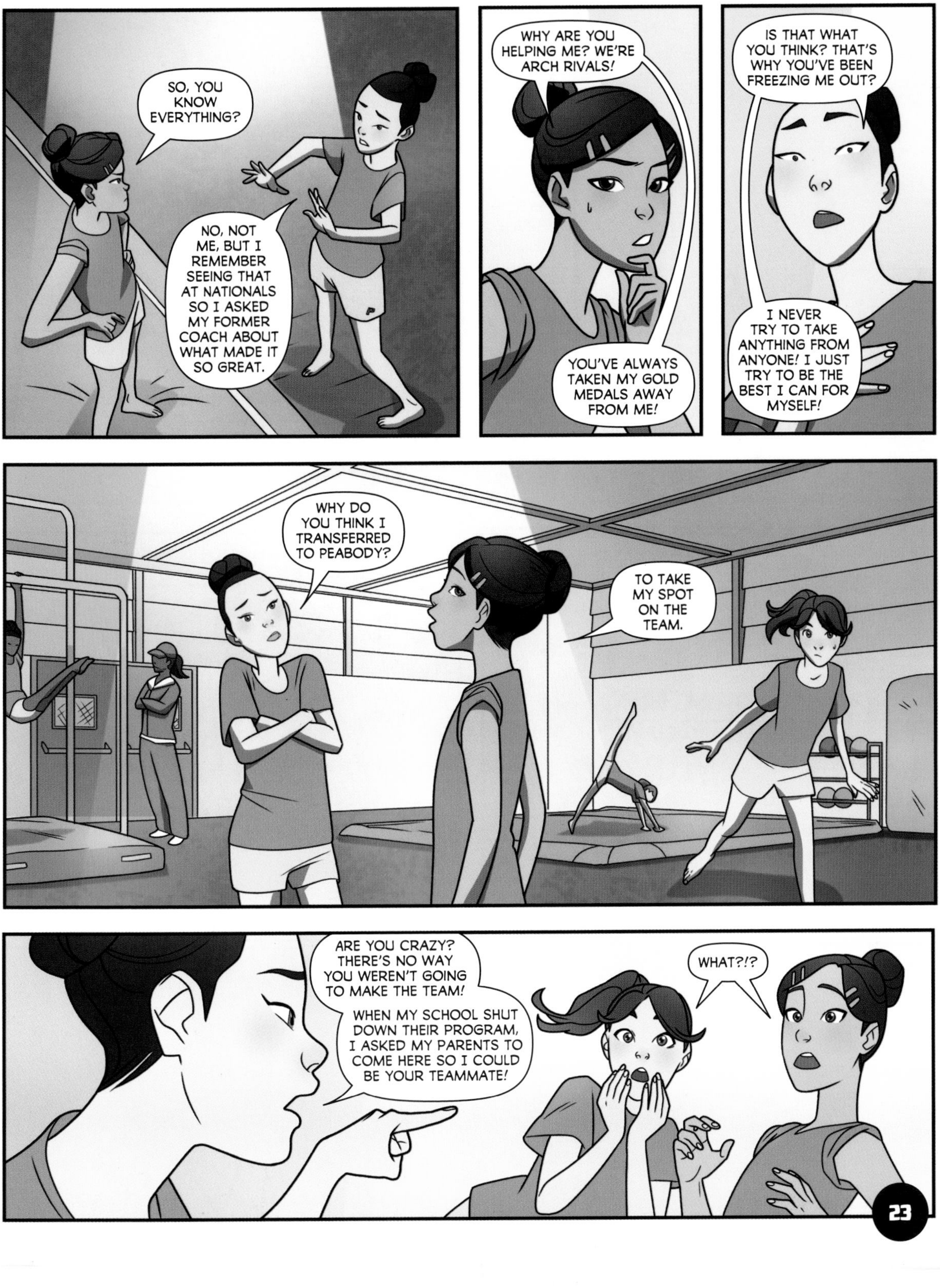
SO, YOU KNOW EVERYTHING?
NO, NOT ME, BUT I REMEMBER SEEING THAT AT NATIONALS SO I ASKED MY FORMER COACH ABOUT WHAT MADE IT SO GREAT.
WHY ARE YOU HELPING ME? WE'RE ARCH RIVALS!
YOU'VE ALWAYS TAKEN MY GOLD MEDALS AWAY FROM ME!
IS THAT WHAT YOU THINK? THAT'S WHY YOU'VE BEEN FREEZING ME OUT?
I NEVER TRY TO TAKE ANYTHING FROM ANYONE! I JUST TRY TO BE THE BEST I CAN FOR MYSELF!
WHY DO YOU THINK I TRANSFERRED TO PEABODY?
TO TAKE MY SPOT ON THE TEAM.
ARE YOU CRAZY? THERE'S NO WAY YOU WEREN'T GOING TO MAKE THE TEAM!
WHEN MY SCHOOL SHUT DOWN THEIR PROGRAM, I ASKED MY PARENTS TO COME HERE SO I COULD BE YOUR TEAMMATE!
WHAT?!?

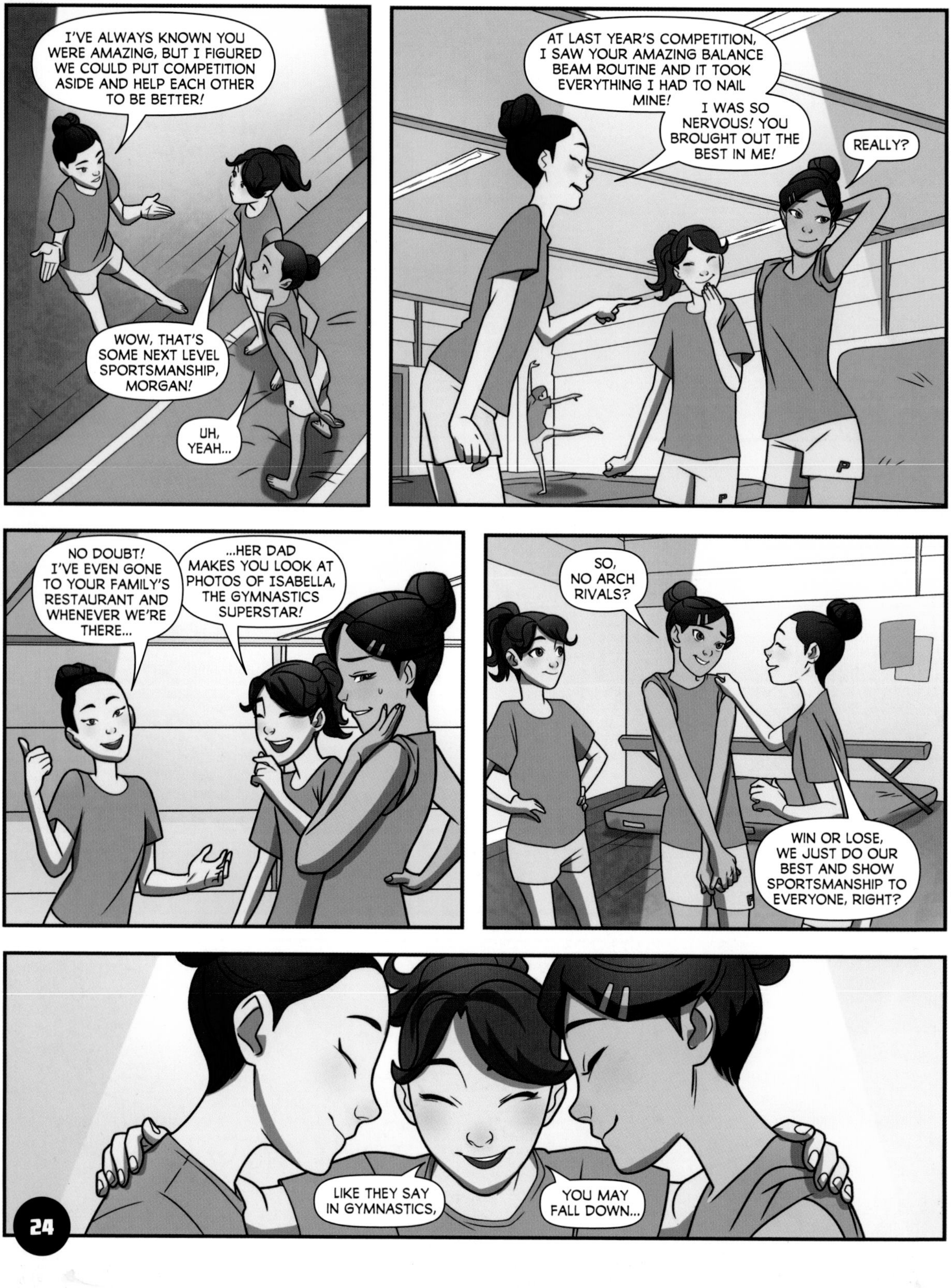
I'VE ALWAYS KNOWN YOU WERE AMAZING, BUT I FIGURED WE COULD PUT COMPETITION ASIDE AND HELP EACH OTHER TO BE BETTER!
WOW, THAT'S SOME NEXT LEVEL SPORTSMANSHIP, MORGAN!
UH, YEAH...
AT LAST YEAR'S COMPETITION, I SAW YOUR AMAZING BALANCE BEAM ROUTINE AND IT TOOK EVERYTHING I HAD TO NAIL MINE!
I WAS SO NERVOUS! YOU BROUGHT OUT THE BEST IN ME!
REALLY?
NO DOUBT! I'VE EVEN GONE TO YOUR FAMILY'S RESTAURANT AND WHENEVER WE'RE THERE...
...HER DAD MAKES YOU LOOK AT PHOTOS OF ISABELLA, THE GYMNASTICS SUPERSTAR!
SO, NO ARCH RIVALS?
WIN OR LOSE, WE JUST DO OUR BEST AND SHOW SPORTSMANSHIP TO EVERYONE, RIGHT?
LIKE THEY SAY IN GYMNASTICS,
YOU MAY FALL DOWN...

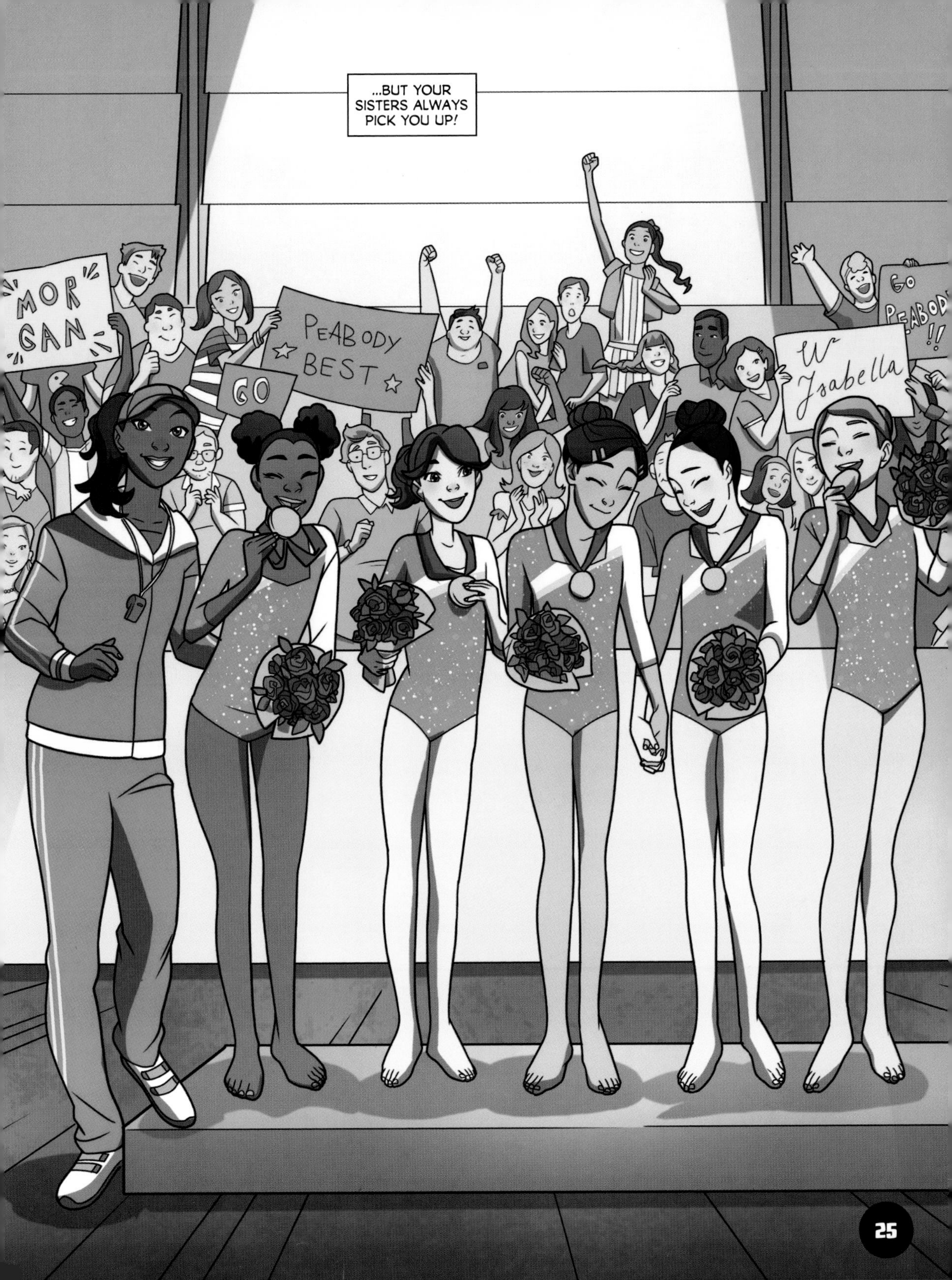
...BUT YOUR SISTERS ALWAYS PICK YOU UP!
MOR GAN
PEABODY BEST
GO
GO PEABODY!!
Isabella

ISABELLA &

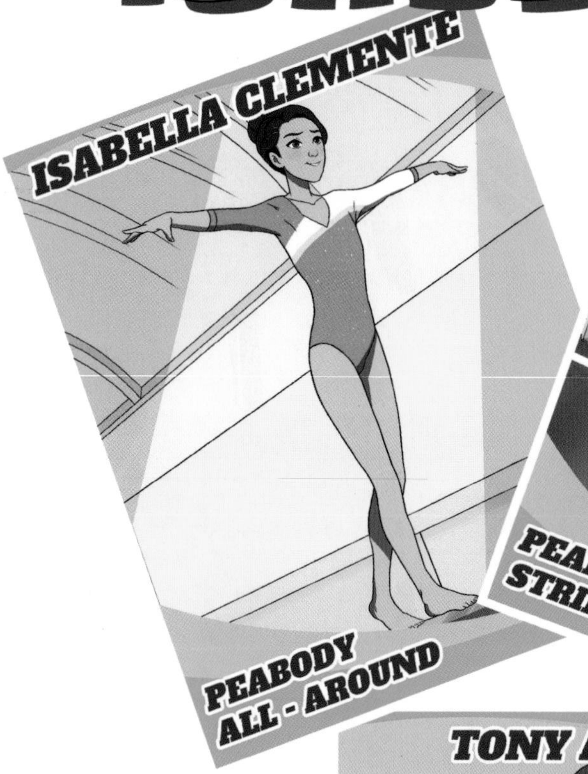
ISABELLA CLEMENTE
PEABODY
ALL - AROUND

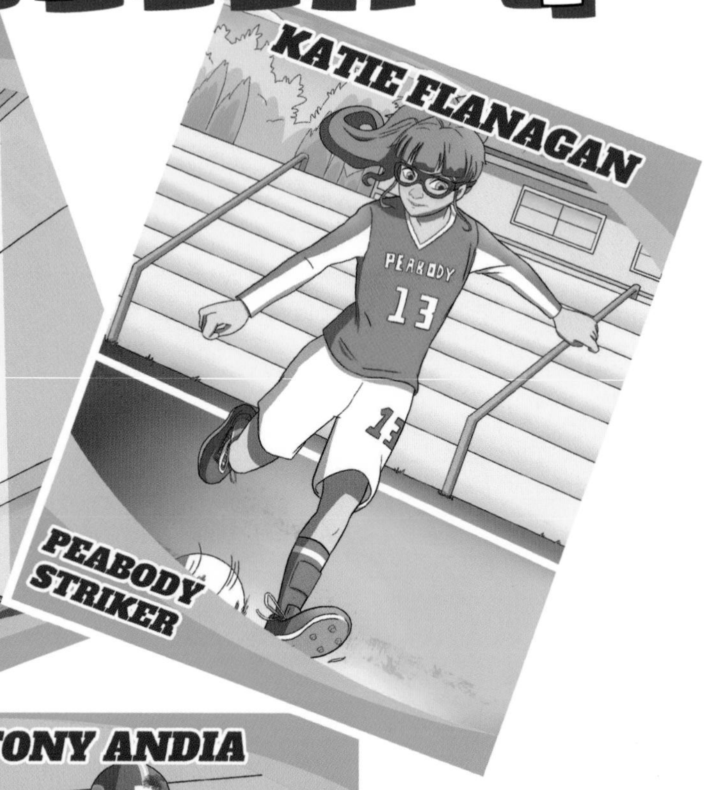
KATIE FLANAGAN
PEABODY
13
PEABODY
STRIKER

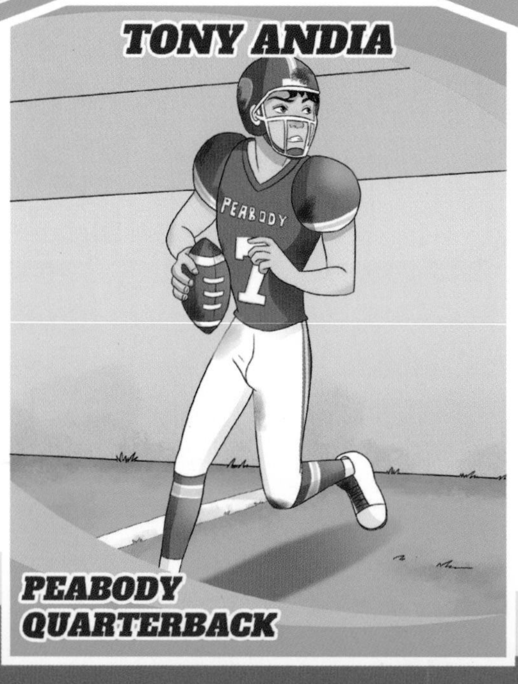
TONY ANDIA
PEABODY
7
PEABODY
QUARTERBACK

FRIENDS

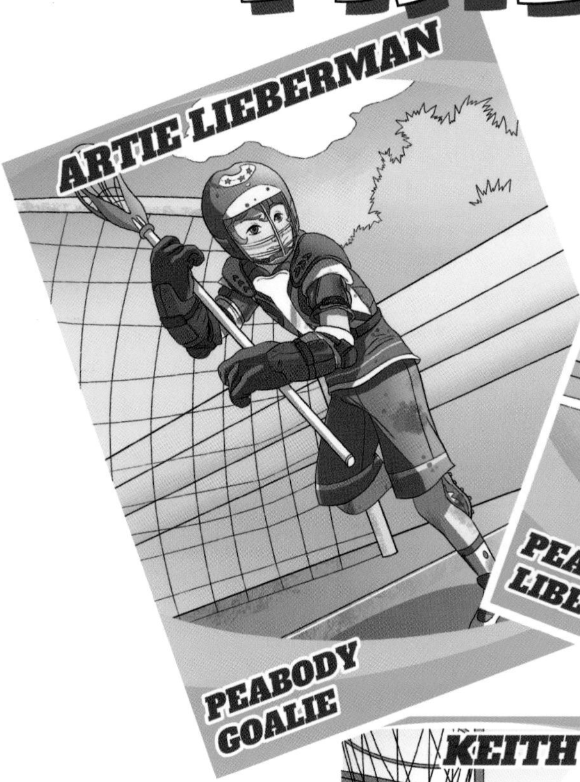
ARTIE LIEBERMAN
PEABODY
GOALIE

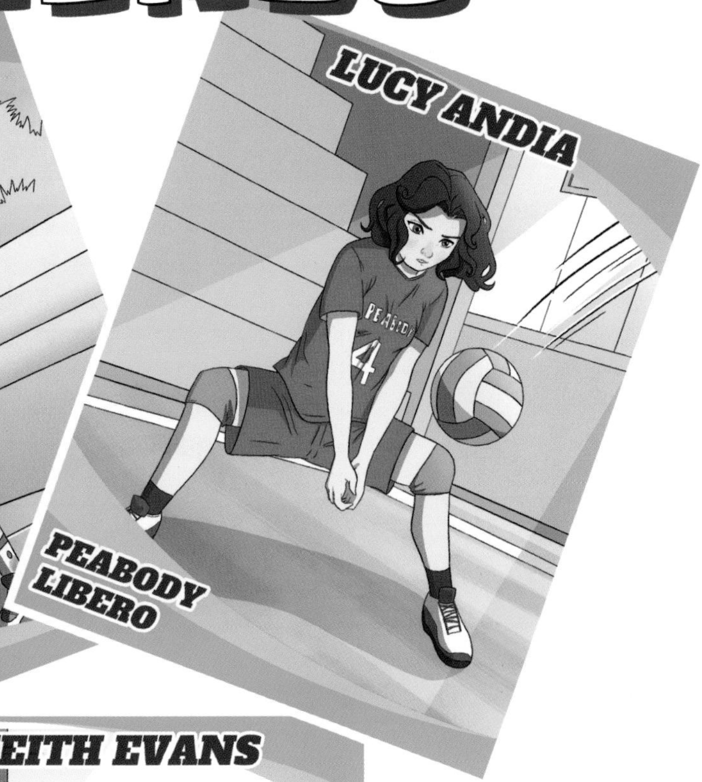
LUCY ANDIA
PEABODY
4
PEABODY
LIBERO

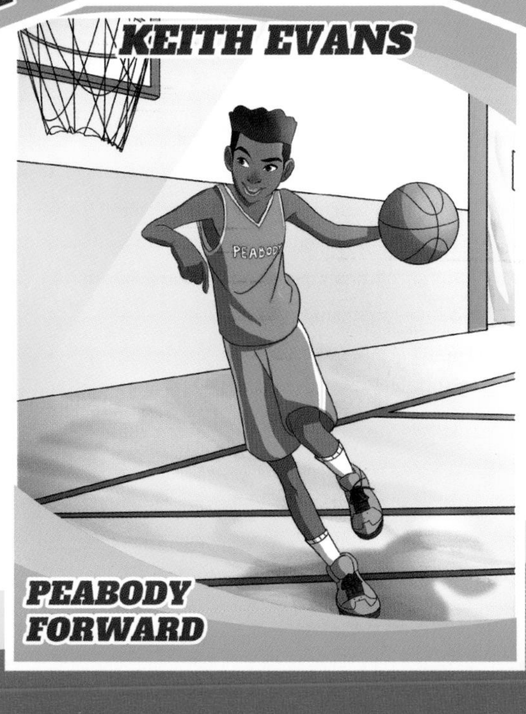
KEITH EVANS
PEABODY
PEABODY
FORWARD

GYMNASTICS

1. Men have competed in gymnastics since the first modern Summer Olympic Games held in Athens in 1896. Women began to compete in which year?

a. 1896
b. 1928
c. 1952
d. 1984

2. In the past, women gymnasts could only compete as a team and were not given individual awards at the Olympics. What year did that finally change?

a. 1896
b. 1928
c. 1952
d. 1984

3. In artistic gymnastics, which are the only events in which both men and women can compete?

a. vault and floor exercise
b. uneven bars and pommel horse
c. parallel bars and balance beam
d. rings and horizontal bars

4. At the 2016 Olympics in Rio de Janeiro, which country did not win a medal in the women's team competition for the first time since the 1976 games in Montreal?

a. Jamaica
b. Chad
c. Romania
d. Japan

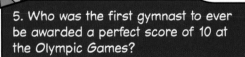

5. Who was the first gymnast to ever be awarded a perfect score of 10 at the Olympic Games?

a. Kerri Strug
b. Mary Lou Retton
c. Nadia Comaneci
d. Simone Biles

QUIZ

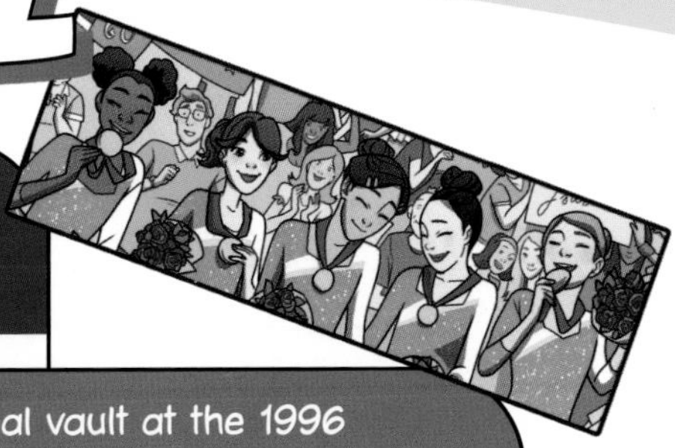

6. Who was the first American woman to win the all-around gold medal at the Olympics?

a. Kerri Strug
b. Mary Lou Retton
c. Gabby Douglas
d. Simone Biles

7. Who completed her final vault at the 1996 Atlanta Olympics on an injured ankle to help the American team win the team all-around gold medal?

a. Kerri Strug
b. Dominique Moceanu
c. Amy Chow
d. Shannon Miller

8. Who was the first African-American woman to win a medal in gymnastics at the Olympics?

a. Dominique Dawes
b. Dominique Moceanu
c. Gabby Douglas
d. Simone Biles

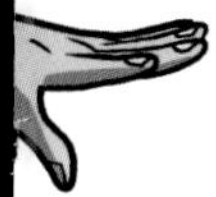

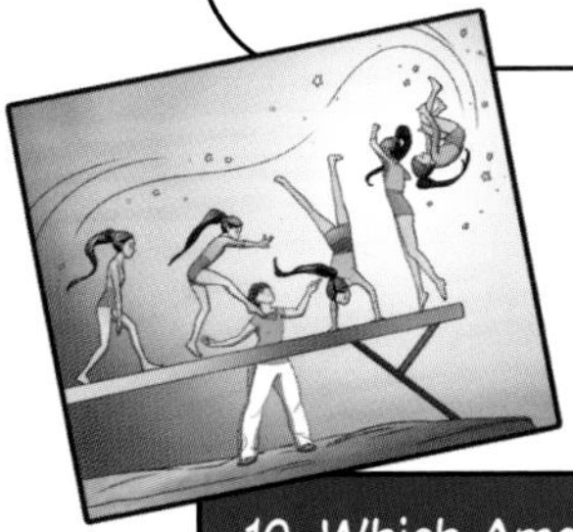

9. Who is considered to be the United States's most successful male gymnast? He was a world champion and earned three Olympic medals including the all-around gold in 2004.

a. Danell Leyva
b. Paul Hamm
c. Jonathan Horton
d. Justin Spring

10. Which American gymnast earned five medals at the 1992 Olympics in Barcelona? She is currently the most decorated American Olympic gymnast with seven medals.

a. Kerri Strug
b. Dominique Moceanu
c. Gabby Douglas
d. Shannon Miller

* Answers on page 32

WHAT DO YOU THINK?

Sportsmanship requires a lot of personal integrity. While you need to do your best and of course it'd be nice to win, you should behave your best towards your teammates and opponents, win or lose.

- Isabella blamed Morgan for her not winning gold medals. Explain if you think that was fair or not. How could she have handled things differently?

- Describe a time when you found it very difficult to accept a loss. How did you react? What could you have done differently?

- Describe a time when you won in a competition but could've demonstrated more sportsmanship to your opponents. What did you do? How did you resolve it?

- How do you think Coach Dawson was trying to teach the girls about teamwork and sportsmanship? How did Isabella's parents try to explain sportsmanship with their restaurant?

- How was Morgan's attitude different than what Isabella thought it was? Describe a time when you may have judged someone unfairly. How did you fix this situation?

GYMNASTICS FUN FACTS

1. The 1996 women's gymnastics team was the first to win the gold medal in the team competition for the United States. Amanda Borden, Amy Chow, Dominique Dawes, Shannon Miller, Dominique Moceanu, Jaycie Phelps, and Kerri Strug were were nicknamed the Magnificent Seven!

2. Bart Conner won gold for the USA in the 1984 Olympic Games in Los Angeles. His wife, Nadia Comaneci is a former Romanian gold medalist. They operate a gymnastics academy in Oklahoma. Talk about learning from the best teachers!

3. Gymnast George Eyser earned six medals in one day during the 1904 Summer Olympics in St. Louis including 3 golds! Even more amazing was that he competed with a wooden prosthetic leg!

4. Kohei Uchimura of Japan earned 7 Olympic medals including the 2016 all-around gold. He also won 19 world gymnastics medals, including 6 world championships! No wonder he is considered to be one of the best male gymnasts of all time!

5. Artistic gymnastics using apparatus or floor exercises have been around since the earliest Olympic Games. Rhythmic gymnastics first appeared at the 1984 games in Los Angeles. Gymnasts on the trampoline first competed in the 2000 Summer Olympic Games in Sydney, Australia.

GLOSSARY

amplitude – The maximum height and power when moving.

dismount – Getting off of something.

stick the landing – Landing with both feet on the ground and little to no movement after completing a gymnastics routine.

ANSWERS

1. b   2. c   3. a   4. d   5. c   6. b   7. a   8. a   9. b   10. d

ONLINE RESOURCES

Booklinks
NONFICTION NETWORK
FREE! ONLINE NONFICTION RESOURCES

To learn more about gymnastics, teamwork, and, sportsmanship visit **abdobooklinks.com**. These links are routinely monitored and updated to provide the most current information available.